W9-CZS-567

Ramona Quimby, Age 8

Beezus and Ramona
Ellen Tebbits
Emily's Runaway Imagination
Fifteen
Henry and Beezus
Henry and the Clubhouse
Henry and the Paper Route
Henry and Ribsy
Henry Huggins
Jean and Johnny
The Luckiest Girl
Mitch and Amy
The Mouse and the Motorcycle
Otis Spofford
Ramona and Her Father
Ramona and Her Mother
Ramona the Brave
Ramona the Pest
The Real Hole
Ribsy
Runaway Ralph
Sister of the Bride
Socks
Two Dog Biscuits

Ramona Quimby, Age 8

BEVERLY CLEARY

ILLUSTRATED BY ALAN TIEGREEN

William Morrow and Company
New York 1981

Printed in the United States of America.
5 6 7 8 9 10

Library of Congress Cataloging in Publication Data

Cleary, Beverly.
    Ramona Quimby, age 8.
    Summary: The further adventures of the Quimby family as Ramona enters the third grade.
    [1. Family life—Fiction] I. Tiegreen, Alan. II. Title.
PZ7.C5792Rais [Fic] 80-28425
ISBN 0-688-00477-6 ISBN 0-688-00478-4 (lib. bdg.)

Contents

Ramona Quimby, Age 8

The First Day of School

Ramona Quimby hoped her parents would forget to give her a little talking-to. She did not want anything to spoil this exciting day.

"Ha-ha, I get to ride the bus to school all by myself," Ramona bragged to her big sister, Beatrice, at breakfast. Her stomach felt quivery with excitement at the day ahead, a day that would begin with a bus ride just the right length to make her feel a long way from home but not

long enough—she hoped—to make her feel carsick. Ramona was going to ride the bus, because
changes had been made in the schools in the
Quimbys' part of the city during the summer.
Glenwood, the girls' old school, had become an
intermediate school, which meant Ramona had
to go to Cedarhurst Primary School.

"Ha-ha yourself." Beezus was too excited to
be annoyed with her little sister. "Today I start
high school."

"*Junior* high school," corrected Ramona, who
was not going to let her sister get away with
acting older than she really was. "Rosemont
Junior High School is not the same as high
school, and besides you have to walk."

Ramona had reached the age of demanding
accuracy from everyone, even herself. All summer, whenever a grown-up asked what grade
she was in, she felt as if she were fibbing when
she answered, "third," because she had not

actually started the third grade. Still, she could not say she was in the second grade since she had finished that grade last June. Grown-ups did not understand that summers were free from grades.

"Ha-ha to both of you," said Mr. Quimby, as he carried his breakfast dishes into the kitchen. "You're not the only ones going to school today." Yesterday had been his last day working at the check-out counter of the Shop-Rite Market. Today he was returning to college to become what he called "a real, live school teacher." He was also going to work one day a week in the frozen-food warehouse of the chain of Shop-Rite Markets to help the family "squeak by," as the grown-ups put it, until he finished his schooling.

"Ha-ha to all of you if you don't hurry up," said Mrs. Quimby, as she swished suds in the dishpan. She stood back from the sink so she would not spatter the white uniform she wore

13

in the doctor's office where she worked as a receptionist.

"Daddy, will you have to do homework?" Ramona wiped off her milk moustache and gathered up her dishes.

"That's right." Mr. Quimby flicked a dish towel at Ramona as she passed him. She giggled and dodged, happy because he was happy.

Never again would he stand all day at a cash register, ringing up groceries for a long line of people who were always in a hurry.

Ramona slid her plate into the dishwater. "And will Mother have to sign your progress reports?"

Mrs. Quimby laughed. "I hope so."

Beezus was last to bring her dishes into the kitchen. "Daddy, what do you have to study to learn to be a teacher?" she asked.

Ramona had been wondering the same thing. Her father knew how to read and do arithmetic. He also knew about Oregon pioneers and about two pints making one quart.

Mr. Quimby wiped a plate and stacked it in the cupboard. "I'm taking an art course, because I want to teach art. And I'll study child development—"

Ramona interrupted. "What's child development?"

15

"How kids grow," answered her father.

Why does anyone have to go to school to study a thing like that? wondered Ramona. All her life she had been told that the way to grow was to eat good food, usually food she did not like, and get plenty of sleep, usually when she had more interesting things to do than go to bed.

Mrs. Quimby hung up the dishcloth, scooped up Picky-picky, the Quimbys' old yellow cat, and dropped him at the top of the basement steps. "Scat, all of you," she said, "or you'll be late for school."

After the family's rush to brush teeth, Mr. Quimby said to his daughters, "Hold out your hands," and into each waiting pair he dropped a new pink eraser. "Just for luck," he said, "not because I expect you to make mistakes."

"Thank you," said the girls. Even a small present was appreciated, because presents of

16

any kind had been scarce while the family tried to save money so Mr. Quimby could return to school. Ramona, who liked to draw as much as her father, especially treasured the new eraser, smooth, pearly pink, smelling softly of rubber, and just right for erasing pencil lines.

Mrs. Quimby handed each member of her family a lunch, two in paper bags and one in a lunch box for Ramona. "Now, Ramona—" she began.

Ramona sighed. Here it was, that little talking-to she always dreaded.

"Please remember," said her mother, "you really must be nice to Willa Jean."

Ramona made a face. "I try, but it's awfully hard."

Being nice to Willa Jean was the part of Ramona's life that was not changing, the part she wished would change. Every day after school she had to go to her friend Howie Kemp's house, where her parents paid Howie's grandmother to look after her until one of them could come for her. Both of Howie's parents, too, went off to work each day. She liked Howie, but after spending most of the summer, except for swimming lessons in the park, at the Kemps' house, she was tired of having to play with four-year-old Willa Jean. She was also tired of apple juice and graham crackers for a snack every single day.

"No matter what Willa Jean does," complained Ramona, "her grandmother thinks it's my fault because I'm bigger. Like the time Willa Jean wore her flippers when she ran under the sprinkler, pretending she was the mermaid on the tuna-fish can, and then left big wet footprints on the kitchen floor. Mrs. Kemp said I should have stopped her because Willa Jean didn't know any better!"

Mrs. Quimby gave Ramona a quick hug. "I know it isn't easy, but keep trying."

18

When Ramona sighed, her father hugged her and said, "Remember, kid, we're counting on you." Then he began to sing, "We've got high hopes, try hopes, buy cherry pie-in-July hopes—"

Ramona enjoyed her father's making up new words for the song about the little old ant moving the rubber tree plant, and she liked being big enough to be counted on, but sometimes when she went to the Kemps' she felt as if everything depended on her. If Howie's grandmother did not look after her, her mother could not work full time. If her mother did not work full time, her father could not go to school. If her father did not go to school, he might have to go back to being a checker, the work that made him tired and cross.

Still, Ramona had too many interesting things to think about to let her responsibility worry her as she walked through the autumn sunshine toward her school bus stop, her new eraser in

19

hand, new sandals on her feet, that quivery feeling of excitement in her stomach, and the song about high hopes running through her head.

She thought about her father's new part-time job zipping around in a warehouse on a fork-lift truck, filling orders for orange juice, peas, fish sticks, and all the other frozen items the markets carried. He called himself Santa's Little Helper, because the temperature of the warehouse was way below zero, and he would have to wear heavy padded clothing to keep from freezing. The job sounded like fun to Ramona. She wondered how she was going to feel about her father's teaching art to other people's children and decided not to think about that for a while.

Instead, Ramona thought about Beezus going off to another school, where she would get to take a cooking class and where she could not come to the rescue if her little sister got into trouble. As Ramona approached her bus stop, she thought about one of the best parts of her new school: none of her teachers in her new school would know she was Beatrice's little sister. Teachers always like Beezus; she was so prompt and neat. When both girls had gone to Glenwood School, Ramona often felt as if teachers were thinking, I wonder why Ramona Quimby isn't more like her big sister.

When Ramona reached the bus stop, she found Howie Kemp already waiting with his grandmother and Willa Jean, who had come to wave good-by.

Howie looked up from his lunch box, which he had opened to see what he was going to have for lunch, and said to Ramona, "Those new sandals make your feet look awfully big."

"Why, Howie," said his grandmother, "that's not a nice thing to say."

Ramona studied her feet. Howie was right, but why shouldn't her new sandals make her feet

look big? Her feet had grown since her last pair.
She was not offended.

"Today I'm going to *kidnergarten*," boasted
Willa Jean, who was wearing new coveralls and
T-shirt and a pair of her mother's old earrings.

Willa Jean was convinced she was beautiful, because her grandmother said so. Ramona's mother said Mrs. Kemp was right. Willa Jean was beautiful when she was clean, because she was a healthy child. Willa Jean did not feel she was beautiful like a healthy child. She felt she was beautiful like a grown-up lady on TV.

Ramona tried to act kindly toward little Willa Jean. After all, her family was depending on her. "Not *kidnergarten*, Willa Jean," she said. "You mean nursery school."

Willa Jean gave Ramona a cross, stubborn look that Ramona knew too well. "I am too going to *kid*nergarten," she said. "*Kid*nergarten is where the kids are."

"Bless her little heart," said her grandmother, admiring as always.

The bus, the little yellow school bus Ramona had waited all summer to ride, pulled up at the curb. Ramona and Howie climbed aboard as if they were used to getting on buses by themselves. I did it just like a grown-up, thought Ramona.

"Good morning. I am Mrs. Hanna, your bus aide," said a woman sitting behind the driver. "Take the first empty seats toward the back." Ramona and Howie took window seats on opposite sides of the bus, which had a reassuring new smell. Ramona always dreaded the people-and-fumes smell of the big city buses.

"By-byee," called Mrs. Kemp and Willa Jean, waving as if Ramona and Howie were going on a long, long journey. "By-byee." Howie pretended not to know them.

As soon as the bus pulled away from the curb, Ramona felt someone kick the back of her seat. She turned and faced a sturdy boy wearing a baseball cap with the visor turned up and a white T-shirt with a long word printed across

the front. She studied the word to see if she could find short words in it, as she had learned to do in second grade. *Earth. Quakes. Earth-quakes.* Some kind of team. Yes, he looked like the sort of boy whose father would take him to ball games. He did not have a lunch box, which meant he was going to buy his lunch in the cafeteria.

A grown-up would not call him a purple cootie. Ramona faced front without speaking. This boy was not going to spoil her first day in the third grade.

Thump, thump, thump against the back of Ramona's seat. The bus stopped for other children, some excited and some anxious. Still the kicking continued. Ramona ignored it as the bus passed her former school. Good old Glenwood, thought Ramona, as if she had gone there a long, long time ago.

"All right, Danny," said the bus aide to the kicking boy. "As long as I'm riding shotgun on this bus, we won't have anyone kicking the seats. Understand?"

Ramona smiled to herself as she heard Danny mutter an answer. How funny—the bus aide saying she was riding shotgun as if she were guarding a shipment of gold on a stagecoach instead of making children behave on a little yellow school bus.

Ramona pretended she was riding a stage-coach pursued by robbers until she discovered her eraser, her beautiful pink eraser, was missing. "Did you see my eraser?" she asked a second-grade girl, who had taken the seat beside her. The two searched the seat and the floor. No eraser.

Ramona felt a tap on her shoulder and turned. "Was it a pink eraser?" asked the boy in the baseball cap.

"Yes." Ramona was ready to forgive him for kicking her seat. "Have you seen it?"

"Nope." The boy grinned as he jerked down the visor of his baseball cap.

That grin was too much for Ramona. "Liar!" she said with her most ferocious glare, and faced front once more, angry at the loss of her new eraser, angry with herself for dropping it so the boy could find it. Purple cootie, she thought, and hoped the cafeteria would serve him fish portions and those canned green beans with the strings left on. And apple wedges, the soft mushy kind with tough skins, for dessert.

The bus stopped at Cedarhurst, Ramona's new school, a two-story red-brick building very much like her old school. As the children hopped out of the bus, Ramona felt a little thrill of triumph. She had not been carsick. She now discovered she felt as if she had grown even more than her feet. Third-graders were the biggest people—except teachers, of course—at this school. All the little first- and second-graders running around the playground, looking so young, made Ramona feel tall, grown-up, and sort of . . . well, wise in the ways of the world.

Danny shoved ahead of her. "Catch!" he

yelled to another boy. Something small and pink flew through the air and into the second boy's cupped hands. The boy wound up as if he were pitching a baseball, and the eraser flew back to Danny.

"You gimme back my eraser!" Encumbered by her lunch box, Ramona chased Danny, who ran, ducking and dodging, among the first- and second-graders. When she was about to catch him, he tossed her eraser to the other boy. If her lunch box had not banged against her knees, Ramona might have been able to grab him. Unfortunately, the bell rang first.

"Yard apes!" yelled Ramona, her name for the sort of boys who always got the best balls, who were always first on the playground, and who chased their soccer balls through other people's hopscotch games. She saw her pink eraser fly back into Danny's hands. "Yard apes!"

she yelled again, tears of anger in her eyes. "Yucky yard apes!" The boys, of course, paid no attention.

Still fuming, Ramona entered her new school and climbed the stairs to find her assigned classroom, which she discovered looked out over roofs and treetops to Mount Hood in the distance. I wish it would erupt, she thought, because she felt like exploding with anger.

Ramona's new room was filled with excitement and confusion. She saw some people she had known at her old school. Others were strangers. Everyone was talking at once, shouting greetings to old friends or looking over those who would soon become new friends, rivals, or enemies. Ramona missed Howie, who had been assigned to another room, but wouldn't you know? That yard ape, Danny, was sitting at a desk, still wearing his baseball cap and tossing Ramona's new eraser from one hand to another.

Ramona was too frustrated to speak. She wanted to hit him. How dare he spoil her day?

"All right, you guys, quiet down," said the teacher.

Ramona was startled to hear her class called "you guys." Most teachers she had known would say something like, "I feel I am talking very loud. Is it because the room is noisy?" She chose a chair at a table at the front of the room and studied her new teacher, a strong-looking woman with short hair and a deep tan. Like my swimming teacher, thought Ramona.

"My name is Mrs. Whaley," said the teacher, as she printed her name on the blackboard. "*W-h-a-l-e-y*. I'm a whale with a *y* for a tail." She laughed and so did her class. Then the whale with a *y* for a tail handed Ramona some slips of paper. "Please pass these out," she directed. "We need some name tags until I get to know you."

Ramona did as she was told, and as she walked among the desks she discovered her new sandals squeaked. *Squeak, creak, squeak.* Ramona giggled, and so did the rest of the class. *Squeak, creak, squeak.* Ramona went up one aisle and down the other. The last person she gave a slip to was the boy from the bus, who was still wearing his baseball cap. "You give me back my eraser, you yard ape!" she whispered.

"Try and get it, Bigfoot," he whispered back with a grin.

Ramona stared at her feet. Bigfoot? Bigfoot was a hairy creature ten feet tall, who was supposed to leave huge footprints in the mountain snows of southern Oregon. Some people thought they had seen Bigfoot slipping through the forests, but no one had ever been able to prove he really existed.

Bigfoot indeed! Ramona's feet had grown,

but they were not huge. She was not going to let him get away with this insult. "Superfoot to you, Yard Ape," she said right out loud, realizing too late that she had given herself a new nickname.

To her astonishment, Yard Ape pulled her eraser out of his pocket and handed it to her with a grin. Well! With her nose in the air, Ramona squeaked back to her seat. She felt so triumphant that she returned the longest way around and bent her feet as much as she could to make the loudest possible squeaks. She had done the right thing! She had not let Yard Ape upset her by calling her Bigfoot, and now she had her eraser in her hand. He would probably call her Superfoot forever, but she did not care. Superfoot was a name she had given herself. That made all the difference. She had won.

Ramona became aware that she was squeaking in the midst of an unusual silence. She stopped midsqueak when she saw her new teacher watching her with a little smile. The class was watching the teacher.

"We all know you have musical shoes," said Mrs. Whaley. Of course the class laughed.

By walking with stiff legs and not bending her feet, Ramona reached her seat without squeaking at all. She did not know what to think. At first she thought Mrs. Whaley's remark was a reprimand, but then maybe her teacher was just trying to be funny. She couldn't tell about grown-ups sometimes. Ramona finally decided that any teacher who would let Yard Ape wear his baseball cap in the classroom wasn't really fussy about squeaking shoes.

Ramona bent over her paper and wrote slowly and carefully in cursive, Ramona Quimby, age 8. She admired the look of what she had written, and she was happy. She liked feeling tall in her new school. She liked—or was pretty sure she liked—her nonfussy teacher. Yard Ape— Well, he was a problem, but so far she had not let him get the best of her for keeps. Besides, although she might never admit it to anyone, now that she had her eraser back she liked him—sort of. Maybe she enjoyed a challenge.

Ramona began to draw a fancy border, all scallops and curliques, around her name. She was happy, too, because her family had been happy that morning and because she was big enough for her family to depend on.

If only she could do something about Willa Jean. . . .

At Howie's House

"Now be nice to Willa Jean," said Mrs. Quimby, as she handed Ramona her lunch box. Grown-ups often forgot that no child likes to be ordered to be nice to another child.

Ramona made a face. "Mother, do you have to say that every single morning?" she asked in exasperation. Deep down inside, where she hid her darkest secrets, Ramona sometimes longed to be horrid to Willa Jean.

"O.K., O.K., I'll try to remember," said Mrs. Quimby with a little laugh. "I know it isn't easy." She kissed Ramona and said, "Cheer up and run along or you'll miss your bus."

Being a member of the Quimby family in the third grade was harder than Ramona had expected. Her father was often tired, in a hurry, or studying on the dining-room table, which meant no one could disturb him by watching television. At school she was still not sure how she felt about Mrs. Whaley. Liking a teacher was important, Ramona had discovered when she was in the first grade. And even though her family understood, Ramona still dreaded that part of the day spent at Howie's house in the company of Mrs. Kemp and Willa Jean.

Those were the bad parts of the third grade. There were good parts, too. Ramona enjoyed riding the bus to school, and she enjoyed keeping Yard Ape from getting the best of her. Then another good part of the third grade began the second week of school.

Just before her class was to make its weekly visit to the school library, Mrs. Whaley announced, "Today and from now on we are going to have Sustained Silent Reading every day."

Ramona liked the sound of Sustained Silent Reading, even though she was not sure what it meant, because it sounded important.

Mrs. Whaley continued. "This means that every day after lunch we are going to sit at our desks and read silently to ourselves any book we choose in the library."

"Even mysteries?" someone asked.

"Even mysteries," said Mrs. Whaley.

"Do we have to give book reports on what we read?" asked one suspicious member of the class.

"No book reports on your Sustained Silent Reading books," Mrs. Whaley promised the class. Then she went on, "I don't think Sustained Silent Reading sounds very interesting, so I think we will call it something else." Here she printed four big letters on the blackboard, and as she pointed she read out, "*D. E. A. R.* Can anyone guess what these letters stand for?"

The class thought and thought.

"Do Everything All Right," suggested someone. A good thought, but not the right answer.

"Don't Eat A Reader," suggested Yard Ape. Mrs. Whaley laughed and told him to try again.

As Ramona thought, she stared out the window at the blue sky, the treetops, and, in the distance, the snow-capped peak of Mount Hood looking like a giant licked ice-cream cone. *R* could stand for *R*un and *A* for And. "Drop Everything And Run," Ramona burst out. Mrs. Whaley, who was not the sort of teacher who expected everyone to raise a hand before speaking, laughed and said, "Almost right, Ramona, but have you forgotten we are talking about reading?"

"Drop Everything And Read!" chorused the rest of the class. Ramona felt silly. She should have thought of that herself.

Ramona decided that she preferred Sustained Silent Reading to DEAR because it sounded more grown-up. When time came for everyone to Drop Everything And Read, she sat quietly doing her Sustained Silent Reading.

How peaceful it was to be left alone in school. She could read without trying to hide her book under her desk or behind a bigger book. She was not expected to write lists of words she did not know, so she could figure them out by skipping and guessing. Mrs. Whaley did not expect the class to write summaries of what they read either, so she did not have to choose easy books to make sure she would get her summary right. Now if Mrs. Whaley would leave her

41

alone to draw, too, school would be almost perfect.

Yes, Sustained Silent Reading was the best part of the day. Howie and Ramona talked it over after school and agreed as they walked from the bus to his house. There they found two of the new friends he had made at Cedarhurst School waiting with their bicycles.

Ramona sat on the Kemps' front steps, her arms clasped around her knees, her Sustained Silent Reading book of fairy tales beside her, and looked with longing at the boys' two bicycles while Howie wheeled his bicycle out of the garage.

Because Howie was kind and because Ramona was his friend, he asked, "Ramona, would you like to ride my bicycle to the corner and back?"

Would she! Ramona jumped up, eager to take a turn.

"Just once," said Howie.

42

Ramona mounted the bicycle and, while the three boys silently watched, teetered and wobbled to the corner without falling off. Having to dismount to turn the bicycle around was embarrassing, but riding back was easier—at least she didn't wobble quite so much—and she managed to dismount as if she were used to doing so. All I need is a little practice, thought Ramona, as Howie seized his bicycle and rode off with his friends, leaving her with nothing to do but pick up her book and join Willa Jean in the house.

Now that Willa Jean was going to nursery school, she was full of ideas. Dressing up was one of them. She met Ramona at the door with an old curtain wrapped around her shoulders. "Hurry up and have your snack," she ordered, while her grandmother sat watching television and crocheting.

The snack turned out to be pineapple juice

and Rye Crisp, a pleasant change for Ramona, even though Willa Jean stood impatiently beside her, watching every swallow until she had finished.

"Now I'll be the lady and you be the dog," directed Willa Jean.

"But I don't want to be a dog," said Ramona.

Willa Jean's grandmother looked up from her crocheting, reminding Ramona with a glance that Ramona's job in the Quimby family was to get along at the Kemps'. Did she have to be a dog if Willa Jean wanted her to then?

"You have to be the dog," said Willa Jean.

"Why?" Ramona kept an eye on Mrs. Kemp as she wondered how far she dared go in resisting Willa Jean's orders.

"Because I'm a beautiful rich lady and I say so," Willa Jean informed her.

"I'm a bigger, beautifuler, richer lady," said Ramona, who felt neither beautiful nor rich, but

45

certainly did not want to crawl around on her hands and knees barking.

"We can't both be the lady," said Willa Jean, "and I said it first."

Ramona could not argue the justice of this point. "What kind of dog am I supposed to be?" she asked to stall for time. She glanced wistfully at her book lying on the chair, the book she was supposed to read at school, but which she was enjoying so much she brought it home.

While Willa Jean was thinking, Mrs. Kemp said, "Sweetheart, don't forget Bruce is coming over to play in a few minutes."

"Bruce who?" asked Ramona, hoping Willa Jean and Bruce would play together and leave her alone to read.

"Bruce who doesn't wee-wee in the sandbox," was Willa Jean's prompt answer.

"Willa Jean!" Mrs. Kemp was shocked. "What a thing to say about your little friend."

Ramona was not shocked. She understood that there must be a second Bruce at Willa Jean's nursery school, a Bruce who did wee-wee in the sandbox.

As things turned out, Ramona was saved from being a dog by the arrival of a small boy whose mother let him out of the car and watched him reach the front door before she drove off.

Willa Jean ran to let him in and introduced him as Ramona expected, "This is Bruce who doesn't wee-wee in the sandbox." Bruce looked pleased with himself.

Mrs. Kemp felt a need to apologize for her granddaughter. "Willa Jean doesn't mean what she says."

"But I don't wee-wee in the sandbox," said Bruce. "I wee-wee in the—"

"Never mind, Bruce," said Mrs. Kemp. "Now what are you three going to play?"

Ramona was trapped.

"Dress up," was Willa Jean's prompt answer. She dragged from the corner a carton piled with old clothes. Willa Jean shoved one of her father's old jackets at Bruce and handed him an old hat and her blue flippers. She unwound the curtain from her shoulders, draped it over her head, and tied it under her chin. Then she hung a piece of old sheet from her shoulders. Satisfied with herself, she handed a torn shirt to Ramona, who put it on only because Mrs. Kemp was watching.

"There," said Willa Jean, satisfied. "I'll be Miss Mousie, the beautiful bride, and Bruce is the frog and Ramona is Uncle Rat, and now we are going to have a wedding party."

Ramona did not want to be Uncle Rat.

"Mr. Frog would a-wooing go," sang Willa Jean. Bruce joined in, "*Hm-m, hm-m.*" Apparently this song was popular in nursery school. Ramona *hm-m*ed too.

"Say it," Willa Jean ordered Bruce.

"Willa Jean, will you marry me?" sang Bruce.

Willa Jean stamped her foot. "*Not* Willa Jean! Miss Mousie."

Bruce started over. "Miss Mousie, will you marry me?" he sang.

"Yes, if Uncle Rat will agree," sang Willa Jean.

"*Hm-m, hm-m.*"

"*Hm-m, hm-m*," hummed all three.

The two nursery-school children looked to Ramona for the next line. Since she did not remember the words used by Uncle Rat to give Mr. Frog permission to marry Miss Mousie, she said, "Sure. Go ahead."

"OK.," said Willa Jean. "Now we will have the wedding party." She seized Bruce and Ramona by the hand. "Take Bruce's other hand," she ordered Ramona.

Ramona found Bruce's hand inside the long sleeve of the old coat. His hand was sticky.

"Now we'll dance in a circle," directed Willa Jean.

Ramona skipped, Willa Jean pranced, and

Bruce flapped. They danced in a circle, tripping on Miss Mousie's train and wedding veil and stumbling over Mr. Frog's flippers until Willa Jean gave the next order. "Now we all fall down."

Ramona merely dropped to her knees while Willa Jean and Bruce collapsed in a heap, laughing. Above their laughter and the sound of the television, Ramona heard the shouts of the boys outside as they rode their bicycles up and down the street. She wondered how much longer she would have to wait until her mother came to rescue her. She hoped she would arrive before Howie's parents came home from work.

Willa Jean scrambled to her feet. "Let's play it again," she said, beaming, convinced of her beauty in her wedding veil. Over and over the three sang, danced, and fell down. As the game went on and on, Ramona grew bored and varied the words she used to give Mr. Frog permission

51

to marry Miss Mousie. Sometimes she said, "See if I care," and sometimes she said, "Yes, but you'll be sorry." Willa Jean did not notice, she was so eager to get to the party part of the game where they all fell down in a heap.

Still the game went on, over and over, with no sign of Bruce and Willa Jean's tiring. Then Beezus came in with an armload of books.

"Hi, Beezus," said Willa Jean, flushed with laughter. "You can play too. You can be the old tomcat in the song."

"I'm sorry, Willa Jean," said Beezus. "I don't have time to be the old tomcat. I have homework I have to do." She settled herself at the dining-room table and opened a book.

Ramona looked at Mrs. Kemp, who smiled and continued crocheting. Why did Ramona have to play with Willa Jean when Beezus did not? Because she was younger. That was why.

Ramona was overwhelmed by the unfairness of it all. Because she was younger, she always had to do things she did not want to do—go to bed earlier, wear Beezus's outgrown clothes that her mother saved for her, run and fetch because her legs were younger and because Beezus was always doing homework. Now she had to get along with Willa Jean—her whole family was depending on her—and Beezus did not.

Once more Ramona looked at her book of fairy tales waiting on the chair beside the front door, and as she looked at its worn cover she had an inspiration. Maybe her idea would work, and maybe it wouldn't. It was worth a try.

"Willa Jean, you and Bruce will have to excuse me now," Ramona said in her politest voice. "I have to do my Sustained Silent Reading." Out of the corner of her eye she watched Mrs. Kemp.

"OK." Willa Jean was not only impressed by

53

a phrase she did not understand, she had Bruce
to boss around. Mrs. Kemp, who was counting
stitches, merely nodded.

Ramona picked up her book and settled herself in the corner of the couch. Beezus caught
her eye, and the two sisters exchanged con-
spiratorial smiles while Willa Jean and Bruce,
now minus Uncle Rat, raced happily around in
a circle screaming with joy and singing, "She'll
be coming 'round the mountain when she
comes!"

Ramona blissfully read herself off into the
land of princesses, kings, and clever youngest
sons, satisfied that the Quimbys had a clever
younger daughter who was doing her part.

The Hard-boiled Egg Fad

With all four members of the family leaving at different times in different directions, mornings were flurried in the Quimby household. On the days when Mr. Quimby had an eight o'clock class, he left early in the car. Beezus left next because she walked to school and because she wanted to stop for Mary Jane on the way.

Ramona was third to leave. She enjoyed these last few minutes alone with her mother now that Mrs. Quimby no longer reminded her she must be nice to Willa Jean.

"Did you remember to give me a hard-boiled egg in my lunch like I asked?" Ramona inquired one morning. This week hard-boiled eggs were popular with third-graders, a fad started by Yard Ape, who sometimes brought his lunch. Last week the fad had been individual bags of corn chips. Ramona had been left out of that fad because her mother objected to spending money on junk food. Surely her mother would not object to a nutritious hard-boiled egg.

"Yes, I remembered the hard-boiled egg, you little rabbit," said Mrs. Quimby. "I'm glad you have finally learned to like them."

Ramona did not feel it necessary to explain to her mother that she still did not like hard-boiled eggs, not even when they had been dyed for Easter. Neither did she like soft-boiled eggs, because she did not like slippery, slithery food.

Ramona liked deviled eggs, but deviled eggs were not the fad, at least not this week.

On the bus Ramona and Susan compared lunches. Each was happy to discover that the other had a hard-boiled egg, and both were eager for lunchtime to come.

While Ramona waited for lunch period, school turned out to be unusually interesting. After the class had filled out their arithmetic workbooks, Mrs. Whaley handed each child a glass jar containing about two inches of a wet blue substance —she explained that it was oatmeal dyed blue. Ramona was first to say "Yuck." Most people made faces, and Yard Ape made a gagging noise.

"OK., kids, quiet down," said Mrs. Whaley. When the room was quiet, she explained that for science they were going to study fruit flies. The blue oatmeal contained fruit-fly larvae. "And why do you think the oatmeal is blue?" she asked.

Several people thought the blue dye was some sort of food for the larvae, vitamins maybe. Marsha suggested the oatmeal was dyed blue so the children wouldn't think it was good to eat. Everybody laughed at this guess. Who would ever think cold oatmeal was good to eat? Yard Ape came up with the right answer: the oatmeal was dyed blue so the larvae could be seen. And so they could—little white specks.

As the class bent over their desks making labels for their jars, Ramona wrote her name on her slip of paper and added, "Age 8," which she always wrote after her signature. Then she drew tiny fruit flies around it before she pasted the label on her very own jar of blue oatmeal and fruit-fly larvae. Now she had a jar of pets.

"That's a really neat label, Ramona," said Mrs. Whaley. Ramona understood that her teacher did not mean tidy when she said "neat,"

but extra good. Ramona decided she liked Mrs. Whaley after all.

The morning was so satisfactory that it passed quickly. When lunchtime came, Ramona collected her lunch box and went off to the cafeteria where, after waiting in line for her milk, she sat at a table with Sara, Janet, Marsha, and other third-grade girls. She opened her lunch box, and there, tucked in a paper napkin, snug between her sandwich and an orange, was her hard-boiled egg, smooth and perfect, the right size to fit her hand. Because Ramona wanted to save the best for the last, she ate the center of her sandwich—tuna fish—and poked a hole in her orange so she could suck out the juice. Third-graders did not peel their oranges. At last it was time for the egg.

There were a number of ways of cracking eggs. The most popular, and the real reason for bringing an egg to school, was knocking the egg against one's head. There were two ways of doing so, by a lot of timid little raps or by one big whack.

Sara was a rapper. Ramona, like Yard Ape, was a whacker. She took a firm hold on her egg, waited until everyone at her table was watching, and *whack*—she found herself with a handful of crumbled shell and something cool and slimy running down her face.

Everyone at Ramona's table gasped. Ramona needed a moment to realize what had happened. Her egg was raw. Her mother had not boiled her egg at all. She tried to brush the yellow yolk and slithery white out of her hair and away from her face, but she only succeeded in making her hands eggy. Her eyes filled with tears of anger, which she tried to brush away with her wrists. The gasps at her table turned into giggles. From another table, Ramona caught a glimpse of Yard Ape grinning at her.

Marsha, a tall girl who always tried to be motherly, said, "It's all right, Ramona. I'll take you to the bathroom and help you wash off the egg."

Ramona was not one bit grateful. "You go away," she said, ashamed of being so rude. She did not want this third-grade girl treating her like a baby.

61

The teacher who was supervising lunch period came over to see what the commotion was about. Marsha gathered up all the paper napkins from the lunch boxes at the table and handed them to the teacher, who tried to sop up the egg. Unfortunately, the napkins did not absorb egg very well. Instead, they smeared yolk and white around in Ramona's hair. Her face felt stiff as egg white began to dry.

"Take her to the office," the teacher said to Marsha. "Mrs. Larson will help her."

"Come on, Ramona," said Marsha, as if Ramona were in kindergarten. She put her hand on Ramona's shoulder because Ramona's hands were too eggy to touch.

Ramona jerked away. "I can go by myself." With that reply, she ran out of the cafeteria. She was so angry she was able to ignore the giggles and the few sympathetic looks of the other children. Ramona was mad at herself for

following a fad. She was furious with Yard Ape for grinning at her. Most of all she was angry with her mother for not boiling the egg in the first place. By the time she reached the office, Ramona's face felt as stiff as a mask.

Ramona almost ran into Mr. Wittman, the principal, which would have upset her even more. He was someone Ramona always tried to avoid ever since Beezus had told her that the way to remember how to spell the kind of principal who was the principal of a school was to remember the word ended in *p-a-l*, not *p-l-e*, because the principal was her pal. Ramona did not want the principal to be her pal. She wanted him to mind his own business, aloof and important, in his office. Mr. Wittman must have felt the same way because he stepped—almost jumped—quickly aside.

Mrs. Larson, the school secretary, took one

look at Ramona, sprang from her desk, and said, "Well, you need a little help, don't you?"

Ramona nodded, grateful to Mrs. Larson for behaving as if eggy third-graders walked into her office every day. The secretary led her into a tiny room equipped with a cot, washbasin, and toilet that adjoined the office.

"Let's see," said Mrs. Larson, "how shall we go about this? I guess the best way is to wash your hands, then dunk your head. You've heard of egg shampoos, haven't you? They are supposed to be wonderful for the hair."

"Yow!" yelped Ramona, when she dipped her head into the washbasin. "The water's cold."

"It's probably a good thing we don't have warmer water," said Mrs. Larson. "You wouldn't want to cook the egg in your hair, would you?" She rubbed and Ramona snuffled. She rinsed and Ramona sniffed. Finally Mrs. Larson said,

"That's the best I can do," and handed Ramona a wad of paper towels. "Dry yourself off the best you can," she said. "You can wash your hair when you get home."

Ramona accepted the towels. As she sat on the cot, rubbing and blotting and seething in humiliation and anger, she listened to sounds from the office, the click of the typewriter, the ring of the telephone, Mrs. Larson's voice answering.

Ramona began to calm down and feel a little better. Maybe Mrs. Kemp would let her wash her hair after school. She could let Willa Jean pretend to be working in a beauty shop and not say anything about her Sustained Silent Reading. One of these days Willa Jean was sure to catch on that she was just reading a book, and Ramona wanted to postpone that time as long as possible.

Toward the end of lunch period, Ramona

heard teachers drift into the office to leave papers or pick up messages from their boxes. Then Ramona made an interesting discovery. Teachers talked about their classes.

"My class has been so good today," said one teacher. "I can hardly believe it. They're little angels."

"I don't know what's the matter with my class today," said another. "Yesterday they knew how to subtract, and today none of them seems able to remember."

"Perhaps it's the weather," suggested another teacher.

Ramona found all this conversation most interesting. She had blotted her hair as best she could when she heard Mrs. Whaley's big cheerful voice speaking to Mrs. Larson. "Here are those tests I was supposed to hand in yesterday," she said. "Sorry I'm late." Mrs. Larson murmured an answer.

Then Mrs. Whaley said, "I hear my little
show-off came in with egg in her hair." She
laughed and added, "What a nuisance."

Ramona was so stunned she did not try to
hear Mrs. Larson's answer. Show-off! Nuisance!
Did Mrs. Whaley think she had broken a raw
egg into her hair on purpose to show off? And
to be called a nuisance by her teacher when
she was not a nuisance. Or was she? Ramona

did not mean to break an egg in her hair. Her mother was to blame. Did this accident make her a nuisance?

Ramona did not see why Mrs. Whaley could think she was a nuisance when Mrs. Whaley was not the one to get her hands all eggy. Yet Ramona had heard her say right out loud that she was a show-off and a nuisance. That hurt, really hurt.

Ramona sat as still as she could with the damp paper towels in her hands. She did not want to risk even the softest noise by throwing them into the wastebasket. Lunch period came to an end, and still she sat. Her body felt numb and so did her heart. She could never, never face Mrs. Whaley again. Never.

Mrs. Larson's typewriter clicked cheerfully away. Ramona was forgotten, which was the way she wanted it. She even wanted to forget herself and her horrible hair, now drying into stiff spikes. She no longer felt like a real person.

The next voice Ramona heard was that of Yard Ape. "Mrs. Larson," he said, as if he had been running in the hall, "Mrs. Whaley said to tell you Ramona didn't come back after lunch."

The typing stopped. "Oh, my goodness," said Mrs. Larson, as she appeared in the doorway. "Why, Ramona, are you still here?"

How was Ramona supposed to answer?

"Run along back to class with Danny," said the secretary. "I'm sorry I forgot all about you."

"Do I have to?" asked Ramona.

"Of course," said Mrs. Larson. "Your hair is almost dry. You don't want to miss class."

Ramona did want to miss class. Forever. The third grade was spoiled forever.

"Aw, come on, Ramona," said Yard Ape, for once not teasing.

Surprised by sympathy from Yard Ape, Ramona reluctantly left the office. She expected him to go on ahead of her, but instead he walked beside her, as if they were friends instead of rivals. Ramona felt strange walking down the hall alone with a boy. As she trudged along beside him, she felt she had to tell someone the terrible news. "Mrs. Whaley doesn't like me," she said in a flat voice.

"Don't let old Whaley get you down," he answered. "She likes you OK. You're a good kid."

Ramona was a little shocked at hearing her teacher called "old Whaley." However, she squeezed comfort from Yard Ape's opinion. She began to like him, really like him.

When they reached their classroom, Yard Ape, perhaps thinking he had been *too* nice to Ramona, turned and said to her with his old grin, "Egghead!"

Oh! There was nothing for Ramona to do but follow him into the room. Sustained Silent Reading, or DEAR, as Mrs. Whaley called it, was

71

over, and class was practicing writing cursive capital letters. Mrs. Whaley was describing capital *M* as she wrote it on the board. "Swoop down, swoop up, down, up again, and down." Ramona avoided looking at her teacher as she got out paper and pencil and began to write the capital letters of the alphabet in careful, even script. She enjoyed the work, and it soothed her hurt feelings until she came to the letter *Q*.

Ramona sat looking at the cursive capital *Q*, the first letter of her last name. Ramona had always been fond of *Q*, the only letter of the alphabet with a neat little tail. She enjoyed printing *Q*, but she did not like her written *Q*. She had made it right, but it looked like a big floppy 2, which Ramona felt was a dumb way to make such a nice letter.

Ramona decided right then and there that she would never again write a cursive *Q*. She would write the rest of her last name, *uimby*, in cursive, but she would always, no matter what Mrs. Whaley said, print her capital *Q*'s.

So there, Mrs. Whaley, thought Ramona. You can't make me write a cursive *Q* if I don't want to. She began to feel like a real person again.

The Quimbys' Quarrel

"But Ramona," said Mrs. Quimby on Saturday, "I've already told you that I boiled several eggs so I wouldn't have to boil an egg for you every morning. I put the boiled eggs on one shelf in the refrigerator and the raw eggs on another. In my hurry, I took an egg from the wrong shelf. I am sorry. There is nothing more I can say."

Ramona remained silent. She felt mean and unhappy because she wanted to forgive her mother, but something in that dark, deep-down place inside her would not let her. Hearing her teacher call her a show-off and a nuisance hurt so much she could not stop being angry at almost everyone.

Mrs. Quimby sighed in a tired sort of way as she gathered up sheets and towels to feed into the washing machine in the basement. Ramona stared out the window and wished the misty rain, which fell softly and endlessly, would go away so she could go outdoors and roller-skate away her bad feelings.

Beezus was no help. She had spent the night at Mary Jane's house with several other girls, and they had stayed up late watching a horror movie on television and eating popcorn. Afterward they stayed awake talking, too scared to go to sleep. That morning Beezus had come home tired and grouchy and had fallen asleep almost immediately.

Ramona wandered around the house looking for something to do, when she discovered her father sitting on the couch, pencil in hand, drawing pad on his knee, frowning at one bare foot.

"Daddy, what are you doing that for?" Ramona wanted to know.

"That's what I keep asking myself," her father answered, as he wiggled his toes. "I have to draw a picture of my foot for my art class."

"I wish we got to do things like that in my school," said Ramona. She found pencil and paper, pulled off one shoe and sock, and climbed on the couch beside her father. Both studied their feet and began to sketch. Ramona soon found that drawing a foot was more difficult than she had expected. Like her father, she stared, frowned, drew, erased, stared, frowned, and drew. For a little while she forgot she was cross. She was enjoying herself.

"There," said Ramona at last. She had drawn

a good, not an excellent, foot. She looked at her
father's paper and was disappointed in what
she saw. It was the kind of picture a teacher
would pin up off in the corner where no one but
the artist would notice it. Her father's foot looked
like a flipper. For the first time, Ramona began

to doubt that her father was the best artist in the whole world. This thought made her feel sad in addition to reminding her she was cross at that world.

Mr. Quimby studied Ramona's picture. "That's not bad," he said. "Not bad at all."

"My foot is easier to draw." Ramona felt as if she should apologize for drawing a better foot than her grown-up father. "My foot is sort of— neater," she explained. "Your foot is kind of bony and your toes are hairy. That makes your foot harder to draw."

Mr. Quimby crumpled his drawing and threw it into the fireplace. "You make me sound like Bigfoot," he said with a rueful laugh, as he threw a cushion at Ramona.

The day dragged on. By dinner time Ramona still had not been able to forgive her mother, who looked even more tired. Mr. Quimby had crumpled several more unsatisfactory drawings of his foot, and Beezus had emerged from her room sleepy-eyed and half-awake, when her mother called the family to supper.

"I wish we could have corn bread again," Ramona said, not because she particularly liked corn bread, but because she felt so cross she wanted to complain about something. Corn bread was a pretty shade of yellow, which would have looked cheerful on a misty day. She leaned forward to sniff the plate of food set before her.

"Ramona." Even though her father did not speak the words, his voice said, "We do not sniff our food in this house."

Ramona sat up. Broccoli and baked potato, both easy to eat. Pot roast. Ramona leaned closer to examine her meat. She could not find one bit of fat, and there was only a bit of gravy poured over her serving. Good. Ramona refused even the tiniest bit of fat. She did not like the slippery, squishy feeling in her mouth.

79

"Delicious," remarked Mr. Quimby, who did not feel he had to inspect his food before eating.

"Nice and tender," said Beezus, beginning to cheer up after her hard night.

Ramona seized her fork, speared her meat to her plate, and began to saw with her knife.

"Ramona, try to hold your fork properly," said her father. "Don't grip it with your fist. A fork is not a dagger."

With a small sigh, Ramona changed her hold on her fork. Grown-ups never remembered the difficulty of cutting meat when one's elbows were so far below the tabletop. She succeeded in cutting a bite of meat the way her parents thought proper. It was unusually tender and not the least bit stringy like some pot roasts her mother had prepared. It tasted good, too. "Yummy," said Ramona, forgetting her anger.

The family ate in contented silence until Beezus pushed aside her gravy with the side of her fork. Gravy was fattening, and although Beezus was slender, even skinny, she was taking no chances.

"Mother!" Beezus's voice was accusing. *"This meat has a rough surface!"*

"It does?" answered Mrs. Quimby innocently.

Ramona understood her mother was trying to hide something when she saw her parents exchange their secret-sharing glance. She too scraped aside her gravy. Beezus was right. One edge of her meat was covered with tiny bumps.

"This meat is tongue." Beezus pushed her serving aside with her fork. "I don't like tongue."

Tongue! Like Beezus, Ramona pushed her meat aside. "Yuck," she said.

"Girls, stop being silly." Mrs. Quimby's voice was sharp.

"What do you mean you don't like tongue?" demanded Mr. Quimby. "You were just eating it and enjoying it."

"But I didn't know it was tongue then," said Beezus. "I hate tongue."

"Me too," said Ramona. "All those yucky little bumps. Why can't we have plain meat?"

Mrs. Quimby was losing patience. "Because tongue is cheaper. That's why. It's cheaper and it's nutritious."

"You know what I think," said Mr. Quimby. "I think this whole thing is a lot of nonsense. You liked tongue when you didn't know it was tongue, so there is no reason why you can't eat it now."

"Yes, this whole thing is ridiculous," said Mrs. Quimby.

"Tongue is disgusting," said Beezus. "Picky-picky can have mine."

"Mine, too," echoed Ramona, knowing she should eat what was set before her, but tongue— Her parents were asking too much.

The meal continued in silence, the girls guilty

but defiant, the parents unrelenting. When Mr. Quimby finished his serving of tongue, he helped himself from Ramona's plate. Picky-picky, purring like a rusty motor, walked into the dining room and rubbed against legs to remind the family that he should eat too.

"I wonder," said Mrs. Quimby, "why we named the *cat* Picky-picky." She and Mr. Quimby looked at one another and only partly suppressed their laughter. The girls exchanged sulky glances. Parents should not laugh at their children.

Beezus silently cleared the table. Mrs. Quimby served applesauce and oatmeal cookies while Mr. Quimby talked about his work as Santa's Little Helper in the frozen-food warehouse. He told how snow fell inside the warehouse door when someone opened it and let in warm air. He told about a man who had to break icicles from his moustache when he left the warehouse.

Snow indoors, icicles on a moustache— Ramona was full of questions that she would not let herself ask. Maybe working as Santa's Little Helper wasn't as much fun as she had thought.

"I'll tell you what," said Mr. Quimby to Mrs. Quimby, when the last cookie crumb had been eaten. "You need a rest. Tomorrow the girls can get dinner and you can take it easy."

"Good idea," said Mrs. Quimby. "Sometimes I do get tired of cooking."

"But I'm supposed to go to Mary Jane's tomorrow," protested Beezus.

"Call her up and tell her you can't come." Mr. Quimby was both cheerful and heartless.

"That's not fair," said Beezus.

"Tell me why it isn't fair," said Mr. Quimby.

When Beezus had no answer, Ramona understood their plight was serious. When their father behaved this way, he never changed his mind. "But I don't know how to cook," Ramona protested. "Except Jello and French toast."

"Nonsense," said Mrs. Quimby. "You are in the third grade, and you can read. Anyone who can read can cook."

"What'll we cook?" Beezus had to accept the fact that she and Ramona had no way out.

"The same things I cook," said her mother. "Whatever I have bought on special that you can find in the refrigerator."

"And corn bread." Mr. Quimby, his face serious but his eyes amused, looked at Ramona. "I expect to be served corn bread."

That evening, after the dishes had been put away, Picky-picky was polishing gravy from his whiskers and their parents were watching the evening news on television. Ramona marched into Beezus's room and shut the door. "It's all

86

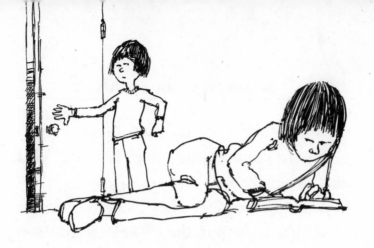

your fault," she informed her sister, who was
lying on the bed with a book. "Why didn't you
keep still?"

"It's just as much your fault," said Beezus.
"You and your yucks."

Both girls recognized nothing would be gained
by arguing over blame.

"But you like to cook," said Ramona.

"And you like to make Jello and French toast,"
said Beezus.

The sisters looked at one another. What had
gone wrong? Why didn't they want to prepare
dinner?

"I think they're mean," said Ramona.

"They're punishing us," said Beezus. "That's what they're doing."

The sisters scowled. They liked to cook; they did not like to be punished. They sat in silence, thinking cross thoughts about parents, especially their parents, their unfair, unkind parents who did not appreciate what nice daughters they had. Lots of parents would be happy to have nice daughters like Beezus and Ramona.

"If I ever have a little girl, I won't ever make her eat tongue," said Ramona. "I'll give her good things to eat. Things like stuffed olives and whipped cream."

"Me too," agreed Beezus. "I wonder what there is for us to cook."

"Let's go look in the refrigerator," suggested Ramona.

Beezus objected. "If they hear us open the refrigerator, Mom and Dad will think we're hungry, and we'll get a lecture on not eating our dinner."

"But I *am* hungry," said Ramona, although she understood the truth of Beezus's words. Oh well, she wouldn't actually starve to death before breakfast. She found herself thinking of French toast, golden with egg under a snowfall of powdered sugar.

"Maybe. . . ." Beezus was thoughtful. "Maybe if we're extra good, they'll forget about the whole thing."

Ramona now felt sad as well as angry. Here she had worked so hard to do her part by getting along at the Kemps', and now her family was not pulling together. Something had gone wrong. Beezus was probably right. The only way to escape punishment was to try being extra good.

"OK." Ramona agreed, but her voice was gloomy. What a dismal thought, being extra good, but it was better than allowing their parents to punish them.

Ramona went to her own room, where she curled up on her bed with a book. She wished something nice would happen to her mother and father, something that would help them forget the scene at the dinner table. She wished her father would succeed in drawing a perfect foot, the sort of foot his teacher would want to hang in the front of the room above the middle of the blackboard. Maybe a perfect foot would make him happy.

And her mother? Maybe if Ramona could forgive her for not boiling the egg she would be happy. In her heart Ramona had forgiven her, and she was sorry she had been so cross with her mother. She longed to go tell her, but now she could not, not when she was being punished.

The Extra-good Sunday

Sunday morning Ramona and Beezus were still resolved to be perfect until dinner time. They got up without being called, avoided arguing over who should read Dear Abby's advice first in the paper, complimented their mother on her French toast, and went off through the drizzly rain to Sunday school neat, combed, and bravely smiling.

Later they cleaned up their rooms without

being told. At lunchtime they ate without complaint the sandwiches they knew were made of ground-up tongue. A little added pickle relish did not fool them, but it did help. They dried the dishes and carefully avoided looking in the direction of the refrigerator lest their mother be reminded they were supposed to cook the evening meal.

Mr. and Mrs. Quimby were good-humored. In fact, everyone was so unnaturally pleasant that Ramona almost wished someone would say something cross. By early afternoon the question was still hanging in the air. Would the girls really have to prepare dinner?

Why doesn't somebody say something? Ramona thought, weary of being so good, weary of longing to forgive her mother for the raw egg in her lunch.

"Well, back to the old foot," said Mr. Quimby, as he once more settled himself on the couch with drawing pad and pencil and pulled off his shoe and sock.

The rain finally stopped. Ramona watched for dry spots to appear on the sidewalk and thought of her roller skates in the closet. She looked into Beezus's room and found her sister reading. Ramona knew Beezus wanted to telephone Mary Jane but had decided to wait until Mary Jane called to ask why she had not come over. Mary Jane did not call. The day dragged on.

When dry spots on the concrete in front of the Quimbys' house widened until moisture remained only in the cracks of the sidewalk, Ramona pulled her skates out of her closet. To her father, who was holding a drawing of his foot at arm's length to study it, she said, "Well, I guess I'll go out and skate."

"Aren't you forgetting something?" he asked.

"What?" asked Ramona, knowing very well what.

"Dinner," he said.

The question that had hung in the air all day was answered. The matter was settled.

"We're stuck," Ramona told Beezus. "Now we can stop being so good."

The sisters went into the kitchen, shut the door, and opened the refrigerator.

"A package of chicken thighs," said Beezus with a groan. "And a package of frozen peas. And yoghurt, one carton of plain and one of

banana. There must have been a special on yoghurt." She closed the refrigerator and reached for a cookbook.

"I could make place cards," said Ramona, as Beezus frantically flipped pages.

"We can't eat place cards," said Beezus. "Besides, corn bread is your job because you brought it up." Both girls spoke in whispers. There was no need to let their parents, their mean old parents, know what was going on in the kitchen.

In her mother's recipe file, Ramona found the card for corn bread written in Mr. Quimby's grandmother's shaky handwriting, which Ramona found difficult to read.

"I can't find a recipe for chicken thighs," said Beezus, "just whole chicken. All I know is that Mother bakes thighs in the flat glass dish with some kind of sauce."

"Mushroom soup mixed with something and with some kind of little specks stirred in." Ramona remembered that much from watching her mother.

Beezus opened the cupboard of canned goods. "But there isn't any mushroom soup," she said. "What are we going to do?"

"Mix up something wet," suggested Ramona. "It would serve them right if it tasted awful."

"Why don't we make something awful?" asked Beezus. "So they will know how we feel when we have to eat tongue."

"What tastes really awful?" Ramona was eager to go along with the suggestion, united with her sister against their enemy—for the moment, their parents.

Beezus, always practical, changed her mind. "It wouldn't work. We have to eat it too, and they're so mean we'll probably have to do the dishes besides. Anyway, I guess you might say our honor is at stake, because they think we can't cook a good meal."

96

Ramona was ready with another solution. "Throw everything in one dish."

Beezus opened the package of chicken thighs and stared at them with distaste. "I can't stand touching raw meat," she said, as she picked up a thigh between two forks.

"Do we have to eat the skin?" asked Ramona. "All those yucky little bumps."

Beezus found a pair of kitchen tongs. She tried holding down a thigh with a fork and pulling off the skin with the tongs.

"Here, let me hold it," said Ramona, who was not squeamish about touching such things as worms or raw meat. She took a firm hold on the thigh while Beezus grasped the skin with the tongs. Both pulled, and the skin peeled away. They played tug-of-war with each thigh, leaving a sad-looking heap of skins on the counter and a layer of chicken thighs in the glass dish.

"Can't you remember what little specks

Mother uses?" asked Beezus. Ramona could not.
The girls studied the spice shelf, unscrewed jar
lids and sniffed. Nutmeg? No. Cloves? Terrible.
Cinnamon? Uh-uh. Chili powder? Well. . . .
Yes, that must be it. Ramona remembered that
the specks were red. Beezus stirred half a tea-
spoon of the dark red powder into the yoghurt,
which she poured over the chicken. She slid the
dish into the oven set at 350 degrees, the temperature for chicken recommended by the cookbook.

From the living room came the sound of their parents' conversation, sometimes serious and sometimes highlighted by laughter. While we're slaving out here, thought Ramona, as she climbed up on the counter to reach the box of cornmeal. After she climbed down, she discovered she had to climb up again for baking powder and soda. She finally knelt on the counter to save time and asked Beezus to bring her an egg.

"It's a good thing Mother can't see you up there," remarked Beezus, as she handed Ramona an egg.

"How else am I supposed to reach things?" Ramona successfully broke the egg and tossed the shell onto the counter. "Now I need buttermilk."

Beezus broke the news. There was no buttermilk in the refrigerator. "What'll I do?" whispered Ramona in a panic.

"Here. Use this." Beezus thrust the carton of

banana yoghurt at her sister. "Yoghurt is sort of sour, so it might work."

The kitchen door opened a crack. "What's going on in there?" inquired Mr. Quimby.

Beezus hurled herself against the door. "You stay out!" she ordered. "Dinner is going to be a—surprise!"

For a moment Ramona thought Beezus had been going to say a mess. She stirred egg and yoghurt together, measured flour, spilling some on the floor, and then discovered she was short of cornmeal. More panic.

"My cooking teacher says you should always check to see if you have all the ingredients before you start to cook," said Beezus.

"Oh, shut up." Ramona reached for a package of Cream of Wheat, because its grains were about the same size as cornmeal. She scattered only a little on the floor.

Something was needed to sop up the sauce

with little red specks when the chicken was served. Rice! The spilled Cream of Wheat gritted underneath Beezus's feet as she measured rice and boiled water according to the directions on the package. When the rice was cooking, she slipped into the dining room to set the table and then remembered they had forgotten salad. Salad! Carrot sticks were quickest. Beezus began to scrape carrots into the sink.

"Yipe!" yelped Ramona from the counter. "The rice!" The lid of the pan was chittering. Beezus snatched a larger pan from the cupboard and transferred the rice.

"Do you girls need any help?" Mrs. Quimby called from the living room.

"No!" answered her daughters.

Another calamity. The corn bread should bake at 400 degrees, a higher temperature than that needed for the chicken. What was Ramona to do?

"Stick it in the oven anyway." Beezus's face was flushed.

In went the corn bread beside the chicken.

"Dessert!" whispered Beezus. All she could find was a can of boring pear halves. Back to the cookbook. "Heat with a little butter and serve with jelly in each half," she read. Jelly. Half a jar of apricot jam would have to do. The pears and butter went into the saucepan. Never mind the syrup spilled on the floor.

"Beezus!" Ramona held up the package of peas.

Beezus groaned. Out came the partially cooked chicken while she stirred the thawing peas into the yoghurt and shoved the dish back into the oven.

The rice! They had forgotten the rice, which was only beginning to stick to the pan. Quick! Take it off the burner. How did their mother manage to get everything cooked at the right

103

time? Put the carrot sticks on a dish. Pour the milk. "Candles!" Beezus whispered. "Dinner might look better if we have candles."

Ramona found two candle holders and two partly melted candles of uneven length. One of them had been used in a Halloween jack o' lantern. Beezus struck the match to light them, because although Ramona was brave about touching raw meat, she was skittish about lighting matches.

Was the chicken done? The girls anxiously examined their main dish, bubbling and brown around the edges. Beezus stabbed a thigh with a fork, and when it did not bleed, she decided it must be done. A toothpick pricked into the corn bread came out clean. The corn bread was done—flat, but done.

Grit, grit, grit sounded under the girls' feet. It was amazing how a tiny bit of spilled Cream of Wheat could make the entire kitchen floor

104

gritty. At last their dinner was served, the din-ing-room light turned off, dinner announced, and the cooks, tense with anxiety that was hid-den by candlelight, fell into their chairs as their parents seated themselves. Was this dinner going to be edible?

"Candles!" exclaimed Mrs. Quimby. "What a festive meal!"

"Let's taste it before we decide," said Mr. Quimby with his most wicked grin.

The girls watched anxiously as their father took his first bite of chicken. He chewed thoughtfully and said with more surprise than necessary, "Why this is good!"

"It really is," agreed Mrs. Quimby, and took a bit of corn bread. "Very good, Ramona," she said.

Mr. Quimby tasted the corn bread. "Just like Grandmother used to make," he pronounced.

The girls exchanged suppressed smiles. They

105

could not taste the banana yoghurt, and by candlelight no one could tell that the corn bread was a little pale. The chicken, Ramona decided, was not as good as her parents thought—or pretended to think—but she could eat it without gagging.

Everyone relaxed, and Mrs. Quimby said chili powder was more interesting than paprika and asked which recipe they had used for the chicken.

Ramona answered, "Our own," as she exchanged another look with Beezus. Paprika! Those little specks in the sauce should have been paprika.

"We wanted to be creative," said Beezus.

Conversation was more comfortable than it had been the previous evening. Mr. Quimby said he was finally satisfied with his drawing, which looked like a real foot. Beezus said her cooking class was studying the food groups everyone should eat every day. Ramona said there was this boy at school who called her Egg-head. Mr. Quimby explained that Egghead was slang for a very smart person. Ramona began to feel better about Yard Ape.

The meal was a success. If the chicken did not taste as good as the girls had hoped and the corn bread did not rise like their mother's, both were edible. Beezus and Ramona were silently grate-ful to their parents for enjoying—or pretend-ing to enjoy—their cooking. The whole family cheered up. When they had finished their pears with apricot jam, Ramona gave her mother a shy smile.

Mrs. Quimby smiled back and patted Ra-mona's hand. Ramona felt much lighter. With-out using words, she had forgiven her mother for the unfortunate egg, and her mother had understood. Ramona could be happy again.

"You cooks have worked so hard," said Mr.

Quimby, "that I'm going to wash the dishes. I'll even finish clearing the table."

"I'll help," volunteered Mrs. Quimby.

The girls exchanged another secret smile as they excused themselves and skipped off to their rooms before their parents discovered the pile of chicken skins and the broken eggshell on the counter, the carrot scrapings in the sink, and the Cream of Wheat, flour, and pear syrup on the floor.

Supernuisance

Once more the Quimbys were comfortable with one another—or reasonably so. Yet Mr. and Mrs. Quimby often had long, serious discussions at night behind their closed bedroom door. The sober sound of their voices worried Ramona, who longed to hear them laugh. However; by breakfast they were usually cheerful—cheerful but hurried.

Ramona was less comfortable at school. In fact, she was most uncomfortable because she was so anxious not to be a nuisance to her teacher. She stopped volunteering answers, and except for the bus ride and Sustained Silent Reading she dreaded school.

One morning, when Ramona was wishing she could get out of going to school, she dug a hole in the middle of her oatmeal with her spoon and watched it fill with milk as she listened to the noise from the garage, the grinding growl of a car that was reluctant to start. "Grr-rrr-rrr," she said, imitating the sound of the motor.

"Ramona, don't dawdle." Mrs. Quimby was whisking about the living room, picking up newspapers, straightening cushions, running a dustcloth over the windowsills and coffee table. Light housekeeping, she called it. Mrs. Quimby did not like to come home to an untidy house.

110

Ramona ate a few spoonfuls of oatmeal, but somehow her spoon felt heavy this morning.

"And drink your milk," said her mother. "Remember, you can't do good work in school if you don't eat a good breakfast."

Ramona paid scant attention to this little speech that she heard almost every morning. Out of habit, she drank her milk and managed most of her toast. In the garage the car stopped growling and started to throb.

Ramona had left the table and was brushing her teeth when she heard her father call in through the back door to her mother, "Dorothy, can you come and steer the car while I push it into the street? I can't get it to go into reverse."

Ramona rinsed her mouth and rushed to the front window in time to see her father put all his strength into pushing the now silent car slowly down the driveway and into the street while her mother steered. At the foot of the driveway, Mrs. Quimby started the motor and drove the car forward beside the curb.

"Now try it in reverse," Mr. Quimby directed.

In a moment Mrs. Quimby called out, "It won't go."

Ramona put on her coat, picked up her lunch box, and hurried out to see what happened when a car would go forward but not backward. She soon discovered her parents found nothing funny about this state of affairs.

"I'll have to take it to the mechanic." Mr. Quimby looked cross. "And then take a bus, which means missing my first class."

"Let me take it, and you hurry and catch a bus now," said Mrs. Quimby. "The answering service can take the doctor's messages a few minutes longer until I get to the office." Then, noticing Ramona standing on the sidewalk, she said, "Run along or you'll miss your bus," and blew Ramona a kiss.

"What if you have to back up?" asked Ramona.

"With luck I won't have to," her mother answered. "Hurry along now."

"So long, Ramona," said Mr. Quimby. Ramona could see that he was more concerned with the car than with her. Perhaps this knowledge made her feet seem heavier than usual as she plodded off to her bus stop. The ride to school seemed longer than usual. When Yard Ape said, "Hi, Egghead," she did not bother to answer, "Deviled Egghead to you," as she had planned.

When school started, Ramona sat quietly filling spaces in her workbook, trying to insert the right numbers into the right spaces but not much caring if she failed. Her head felt heavy, and her fingers did not want to move. She thought of telling Mrs. Whaley that she did not feel good, but her teacher was busy writing a list of words on the blackboard and would probably think anyone who interrupted was a nuisance.

Ramona propped her head on her fist, looking at twenty-six glass jars of blue oatmeal. *Oh-h-h.* She did not want to think about blue oatmeal or white oatmeal or any oatmeal at all. She sat motionless, hoping the terrible feeling would go away. She knew she should tell her teacher, but by now Ramona was too miserable even to raise her hand. If she did not move, not even her little finger or an eyelash, she might feel better.

Go away, blue oatmeal, thought Ramona, and then she knew that the most terrible, horrible, dreadful, awful thing that could happen was going to happen. Please, God, don't let me. . . . Ramona prayed too late.

The terrible, horrible, dreadful, awful thing happened. Ramona threw up. She threw up right there on the floor in front of everyone. One second her breakfast was where it belonged. Then everything in her middle seemed to go into reverse, and there was her breakfast on the floor.

Ramona had never felt worse in her whole life. Tears of shame welled in her eyes as she was aware of the shock and horror of everyone around her. She heard Mrs. Whaley say, "Oh, dear—Marsha, take Ramona to the office. Danny, run and tell Mr. Watts that someone threw up. Children, you may hold your noses and file into the hall until Mr. Watts comes and cleans up."

Her instructions made Ramona feel even worse. Tears streamed down her face, and she longed for Beezus, now far away in junior high school, to come and help her. She let Marsha guide her down the steps and through the hall as the rest of her class, noses pinched between thumbs and forefingers, hurried out of the classroom.

"It's all right, Ramona," Marsha said gently, while keeping her distance as if she expected Ramona to explode.

Ramona was crying too hard to answer. No-

body, nobody in the whole world, was a bigger nuisance than someone who threw up in school. Until now she thought Mrs. Whaley had been unfair when she called her a nuisance, but now —there was no escaping the truth—she really *was* a nuisance, a horrible runny-nosed nuisance with nothing to blow her nose on.

When Ramona and Marsha entered the office, Marsha was eager to break the news. "Oh, Mrs. Larson," she said, "Ramona threw up." Even the principal, sitting at his desk in the inner office, heard the news. Ramona knew he would not come out and start being her pal, because

nobody wanted to be a pal to someone who threw up.

Mrs. Larson, seizing a Kleenex from a box on her desk, sprang from her typewriter. "Too bad," she said calmly, as if throwers-up came into the office every day. "Blow," she directed, as she held the Kleenex to Ramona's nose. Ramona blew. The principal, of course, stayed in his office where he was safe.

Mrs. Larson then took Ramona into the little room off the office, the same room in which she had washed egg out of Ramona's hair. She handed Ramona a paper cup of water. "You want to rinse your mouth, don't you?" Ramona nodded, rinsed, and felt better. Mrs. Larson did not behave as if she were a nuisance.

The school secretary laid a sheet of clean paper on the pillow on the cot, motioned Ramona to lie down, and then covered her with a blanket. "I'll phone your mother and ask her to come and take you home," she said.

"But she's at work," Ramona whispered, because speaking aloud might send her stomach into reverse again. "And Daddy is at school."

"I see," said Mrs. Larson. "Where do you go after school?"

"To Howie Kemp's house," said Ramona, closing her eyes and wishing she could go to sleep and not wake up until all this misery was over. She was aware that Mrs. Larson dialed a number and after a few moments replaced the receiver. Howie's grandmother was not home.

Then the terrible, horrible, dreadful, awful feeling returned. "Mrs. L-Larson," quavered Ramona. "I'm going to throw up."

In an instant, Mrs. Larson was holding Ramona's head in front of the toilet. "It's a good thing I have three children of my own so I'm

119

used to this sort of thing," she said. When Ramona had finished, she handed her another cup of water and said cheerfully, "You must feel as if you've just thrown up your toenails."

Ramona managed a weak and wavery smile. "Who's going to take care of me?" she asked, as Mrs. Larson covered her with the blanket once more.

"Don't worry," said Mrs. Larson. "We'll find someone, and until we do, you rest right here."

Ramona felt feeble, exhausted, and grateful to Mrs. Larson. Closing her eyes had never felt so good, and the next thing she knew she heard her mother whispering, "Ramona." She lifted heavy lids to see her mother standing over her.

"Do you feel like going home?" Mrs. Quimby asked gently. She was already holding Ramona's coat.

Tears filled Ramona's eyes. She was not sure her legs would stand up, and how would they get home without a car? And what was her mother doing here when she was supposed to be at work? Would she lose her job?

Mrs. Quimby helped Ramona to her feet and draped her coat over her shoulders. "I have a taxi waiting," she said, as she guided Ramona toward the door.

Mrs. Larson looked up from her typewriter. " 'Bye, Ramona. We'll miss you," she said. "I hope you'll feel better soon."

Ramona had forgotten what it was like to feel better. Outside a yellow taxicab was chugging at the curb. A taxi! Ramona had never ridden in a taxicab, and now she was too sick to enjoy it. Any other time she would have felt important to be leaving school in a taxi in the middle of the morning.

As Ramona climbed in, she saw the driver look her over as if he were doubtful about something. I will not throw up in a taxi, Ramona

willed herself. I will not. A taxi is too expensive
to throw up in. She added silent words to God,
Don't let me throw up in a taxi.

Carefully Ramona laid her head in her
mother's lap and with every click of the meter
thought, I will not throw up in a taxi. And she
did not. She managed to wait until she was
home and in the bathroom.

How good Ramona's bed felt with its clean white sheets. She let her mother wipe her face and hands with a cool washcloth and later take her temperature. Afterward, Ramona did not care about much of anything.

Late in the afternoon she awoke when Beezus whispered, "Hi," from the doorway.

When Mr. Quimby came home, he too paused in the doorway. "How's my girl?" he inquired softly.

"Sick," answered Ramona, feeling pitiful.

"How's the car?"

"Still sick," answered her father. "The mechanic was so busy he couldn't work on it today."

In a while Ramona was aware that her family was eating dinner without her, but she did not care. Later Mrs. Quimby took Ramona's temperature again, propped her up, and held a glass of fizzy drink to her lips, which surprised Ramona. Her mother did not approve of junk foods.

"I talked to the pediatrician," Mrs. Quimby explained, "and she said to give you this because you need fluids."

The drink gave Ramona a sneezy feeling in her nose. She waited anxiously. Would it stay down? Yes. She sipped again, and in a moment again.

"Good girl," whispered her mother.

Ramona fell back and turned her face into her pillow. Remembering what had happened at school, she began to cry.

"Dear heart," said her mother. "Don't cry. You just have a touch of stomach flu. You'll feel better in a day or so."

Ramona's voice was muffled. "No, I won't."

"Yes, you will." Mrs. Quimby patted Ramona through the bedclothes.

Ramona turned enough to look at her mother

with one teary eye. "You don't know what happened," she said.

Mrs. Quimby looked concerned. "What happened?"

"I threw up on the floor in front of the whole class," sobbed Ramona.

Her mother was reassuring. "Everybody knows you didn't throw up on purpose, and you certainly aren't the first child to do so." She thought a moment and said, "But you should have told Mrs. Whaley you didn't feel good."

Ramona could not bring herself to admit her teacher thought she was a nuisance. She let out a long, quavery sob.

Mrs. Quimby patted Ramona again and turned out the light. "Now go to sleep," she said, "and you'll feel better in the morning."

Ramona was sure that, although her stomach might feel better in the morning, the rest of her would still feel terrible. She wondered what nickname Yard Ape would give her this time and what Mrs. Whaley said to the school secretary about her at lunchtime. As she fell asleep, she decided she was a supernuisance, and a sick one at that.

The Patient

During the night Ramona was half awakened when her mother wiped her face with a cool washcloth and lifted her head from the pillow to help her sip something cold. Later, as the shadows of the room were fading, Ramona had to hold a thermometer under her tongue for what seemed like a long time. She felt safe, knowing her mother was watching over her. Safe but sick. No sooner did she find a cool place on her pillow than it became too hot for comfort, and Ramona turned again.

As her room grew light, Ramona dozed off, faintly aware that her family was moving quietly so they would not disturb her. One tiny corner of her mind was pleased by this consideration. She heard breakfast sounds, and then she must have fallen completely asleep, because the next thing she knew she was awake and the house was silent. Had they all gone off and left her? No, someone was moving quietly in the kitchen. Howie's grandmother must have come to stay with her.

Ramona's eyes blurred. Her family had all gone off and left her when she was sick. She blinked away the tears and discovered on her bedside table a cartoon her father had drawn for her. It showed Ramona leaning against one tree and the family car leaning against another. He had drawn her with crossed eyes and a

turned-down mouth. The car's headlights were crossed and its front bumper turned down like Ramona's mouth. They both looked sick. Ramona discovered she remembered how to smile. She also discovered she felt hot and sweaty instead of hot and dry. For a moment she struggled to sit up and then fell back on her pillow. Sitting up was too much work. She longed for her mother, and suddenly, as if her wish were granted, her mother was entering the bedroom with a basin of water and a towel.

"Mother!" croaked Ramona. "Why aren't you at work?"

"Because I stayed home to take care of you," Mrs. Quimby answered, as she gently washed Ramona's face and hands. "Feeling better?"

"Sort of." In some ways Ramona felt better, but she also felt sweaty, weak, and worried. "Are you going to lose your job?" she asked, remembering the time her father had been out of work.

"No. The receptionist who retired was glad to come in for a few days to take my place." Mrs. Quimby gave Ramona a sponge bath and helped her into cool, dry pajamas. "There," she said. "How about some tea and toast?"

"Grown-up tea?" asked Ramona, relieved that her mother's job was safe so that her father wouldn't have to drop out of school.

"Grown-up tea," answered her mother, as she propped Ramona up with an extra pillow. In a few minutes she brought a tray that held a slice of dry toast and a cup of weak tea.

Nibbling and sipping left Ramona tired and gloomy.

"Cheer up," said Mrs. Quimby, when she came to remove the tray. "Your temperature is down, and you're going to be all right."

Ramona did feel a little better. Her mother was right. She had not thrown up on purpose. Other children had done the same thing. There was that boy in kindergarten and the girl in first grade. . . .

Ramona dozed off, and when she awoke, she was bored and cranky. She wanted butter on the toast her mother brought her and scowled when her mother said people with stomach flu should not eat butter.

Mrs. Quimby smiled and said, "I can tell you're beginning to get well when you act like a wounded tiger."

Ramona scowled. "I am *not* acting like a wounded tiger," she informed her mother. When Mrs. Quimby made her a bed on the living-room couch so she could watch television, she was cross with the television set because she found daytime programs dumb, stupid, and boring. Commercials were much more interesting than the programs. She lay back and hoped for a cat food commercial because she liked to look at nice cats. As she waited, she brooded about her teacher.

"Of course I didn't throw up on purpose," Ramona told herself. Mrs. Whaley should know that. And deep down inside I am really a nice person, she comforted herself. Mrs. Whaley should know that, too.

"Who pays teachers?" Ramona suddenly

asked, when her mother came into the room.

"Why, we all do." Mrs. Quimby seemed surprised by the question. "We pay taxes, and teachers' salaries come out of tax money."

Ramona knew that taxes were something unpleasant that worried parents. "I think you should stop paying taxes," Ramona informed her mother.

Mrs. Quimby looked amused. "I wish we could—at least until we finish paying for the room we added to the house. Whatever put such an idea into your head?"

"Mrs. Whaley doesn't like me," Ramona answered. "She is supposed to like me. It's her job to like me."

All Mrs. Quimby had to say was, "If you're this grouchy at school, liking you could be hard work."

Ramona was indignant. Her mother was supposed to feel sorry for her poor, weak little girl.

Picky-picky strolled into the living room and stared at Ramona as if he felt she did not belong on the couch. With an arthritic leap, he jumped up beside her on the blanket, washed himself from his ears to the tip of his tail, kneaded the blanket, and, purring, curled up beside Ramona, who lay very still so he would not go away. When he was asleep, she petted him gently. Picky-picky usually avoided her because she was noisy, or so her mother said.

A funny man appeared on the television screen. He had eaten a pizza, which had given him indigestion. He groaned. "I can't believe I ate the *whole* thing." Ramona smiled.

The next commercial showed a cat stepping back and forth in a little dance. "Do you think we could train Picky-picky to do that?" Ramona asked her mother.

Mrs. Quimby was amused at the idea of old Picky-picky dancing. "I doubt it," she said. "That

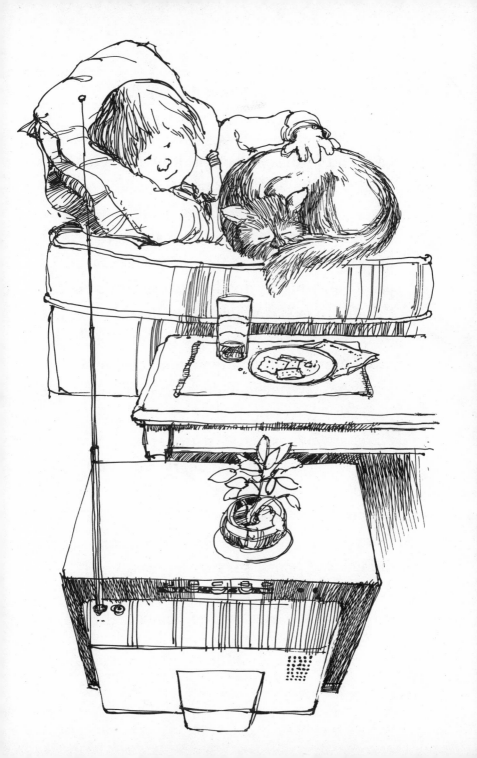

cat isn't really dancing. They just turn the film back and forth so it looks as if he's dancing."

How disappointing. Ramona dozed while another cat-food commercial appeared. She awoke enough to watch a big yellow cat ignore several brands of cat food before he settled down to eat a bowl of dry food silently. That's funny, thought Ramona. When Picky-picky ate dry cat food, he ground and crunched so noisily she could hear him from any room in the house, but television cats never made any sound at all when they ate. The commercials lied. That's what they did. Ramona was cross with cat-food commercials. Cheaters! She was angry with the whole world.

Late that afternoon Ramona was aroused once more by the doorbell. Was it someone interesting? She hoped so, for she was bored. The visitor turned out to be Sara.

Ramona lay back on her pillow and tried to

look pale and weak as her mother said, "Why, hello, Sara. I'm glad to see you, but I don't think you should come in until Ramona is feeling better."

"That's all right," said Sara. "I just brought some letters the class wrote to Ramona, and Mrs. Whaley sent a book for her to read."

"Hi, Sara," said Ramona with the weakest smile she could manage.

"Mrs. Whaley said to tell you this book is not for DEAR. This one is for a book report," Sara explained from the doorway.

Ramona groaned.

"She said to tell you," Sara continued, "that she wants us to stand up in front of the class and pretend we are selling the book. She doesn't want us to tell the whole story. She says she has already heard all the stories quite a few times."

Ramona felt worse. Not only would she have to give a book report, she would have to listen to twenty-five book reports given by other people, another reason for wanting to stay home.

When Sara left, Ramona examined the big envelope she had brought. Mrs. Whaley had written Ramona's name on the front with a floppy cursive capital Q and beneath it in her big handwriting, "Miss you!" followed by a picture of a whale and a y.

I bet she doesn't mean it, thought Ramona. She opened the envelope of the first letters anyone had ever written to her. "Mother, they wrote in cursive!" she cried, delighted. Although all the letters said much the same thing—we are sorry you are sick and hope you get well soon—they made Ramona feel good. She knew they were written to teach letter writing and handwriting at the same time, but she didn't care.

One letter was different. Yard Ape had written, "Dear Superfoot, Get well or I will eat your eraser." Ramona smiled because his letter

showed he liked her. She looked forward to the
return of her father and sister so she could
show off her mail.

Bored with television and cramped from lying
still so she would not disturb Picky-picky, Ramona waited. How sorry they would be to see

her so pale and thin. Surely her father would bring her a little present, something to entertain her while she had to stay in bed. A paperback book because she could now read books with chapters? New crayons? Her father understood the importance of sharp-pointed crayons to someone who liked to draw.

Beezus arrived first with an armload of books that she dropped on a chair. "Homework!" she said and groaned. Now that she was in junior high school, she was always talking about all the work she had to do, as if Ramona did nothing in school. "How do you feel?" she finally got around to asking.

"Sick," said Ramona in a faint voice, "but my whole class wrote to me."

Beezus glanced at the sheaf of letters. "They copied them off the blackboard," she said.

"Writing a whole letter in cursive is hard work for lots of people when they are in the third grade." Ramona was hurt at having her letters belittled. She pushed Picky-picky off the couch so she could stretch her legs. The television droned on and on.

"I wonder what's keeping your father," remarked Mrs. Quimby, looking out the front window.

Ramona knew why her father was late, but she did not say so. He was buying her a little present because she was sick. She could hardly wait. "My class is giving book reports," she informed Beezus, so her sister would know she had schoolwork to do too. "We have to pretend to sell a book to someone."

"We did that a couple of times," said Beezus. "Teachers always tell you not to tell the whole story, and half the kids finish by saying, 'If you want to know what happens next, read the book,' and somebody always says, 'Read this book, or I'll punch you in the nose.'"

Ramona knew who would say that in her class. Yard Ape, that was who.

"Here he comes now," said Mrs. Quimby, and she hurried to open the door for Ramona's father, who kissed her as he entered.

"Where's the car?" she asked.

"Bad news." Mr. Quimby sounded tired. "It has to have a new transmission."

"Oh, no!" Mrs. Quimby was shocked. "How much is that going to cost?"

Mr. Quimby looked grim. "Plenty. More than we can afford."

"We'll have to afford it somehow," said Mrs. Quimby. "We can't manage without a car."

"The transmission people are letting us pay it off in installments," he explained, "and I'll manage to get in some more hours as Santa's Little Helper at the warehouse."

"I wish there were some other way. . . ."

Mrs. Quimby looked sad as she went into the kitchen to attend to supper.

Only then did Mr. Quimby turn his attention to Ramona. "How's my little punkin?" he asked.

"Sick." Ramona forgot to look pitiful, she was so disappointed that her father had not brought her a present.

"Cheer up," Mr. Quimby half smiled. "At least you don't need a new transmission, and you'll feel better tomorrow."

"What's a transmission?" asked Ramona.

"That's what makes the car go," explained her father.

"Oh," said Ramona. Then to show her father that her life was not so easy, she added, "I have to give a book report at school."

"Well, make it interesting," said Mr. Quimby, as he went off to wash for supper.

Ramona knew her father was worried, but

she could not help thinking he might have felt sorrier for his sick little girl. Anyone would think he loved the car more. She lay back genuinely weak, exhausted by television, and sorry her father would have to work more hours in the frozen-food warehouse where, no matter how many pair of woolen socks he wore, his feet were always cold and he sometimes had to go outside until feeling came back into his cheeks.

When her mother, after serving the rest of the family, said the time had come for Ramona to get into her own bed and have a little supper on a tray, she was ready to go. The thought that her mother did not think she was a nuisance comforted her.

Ramona's Book Report

The Quimby family was full of worries. The parents were worried about managing without a car while a new transmission was installed and even more worried about paying for it. Beezus was worried about a party she had been invited to, because boys had also been invited. She was afraid it would turn out to be a dancing party, and she felt silly trying to dance. Besides, eighth-grade boys acted like a bunch of little kids at parties. Ramona, still feeling weak, moped around the house for another day worrying about her book report. If she made it interesting, Mrs. Whaley would think she was showing off. If she did not make it interesting, her teacher would not like it.

On top of everything, Beezus happened to look at her father's head as he bent over his books at the dining-room table that evening. "Daddy, you're getting thin on top!" she cried out, shocked.

Ramona rushed to look. "Just a little thin," she said, because she did not want her father's feelings hurt. "You aren't bald yet."

Mrs. Quimby also examined the top of her husband's head. "It *is* a little thin," she agreed, and kissed the spot. "Never mind. I found a gray hair last week."

"What is this? A conference about my hair?" asked Mr. Quimby, and he grabbed his wife

around the waist. "Don't worry," he told her.
"I'll still love you when you're old and gray."

"Thanks a lot," said Mrs. Quimby, not wanting to think of herself as old and gray. They
both laughed. Mr. Quimby released his wife
and gave her a playful slap on the bottom, an
act that amused and shocked his daughters.

Ramona had two feelings about this conversation. She did not want her father's hair to grow thin or her mother's hair to grow gray. She wanted her parents to stay exactly as they were for ever and ever. But oh, how good it was to see them be so affectionate with one another. She knew her mother and father loved one another, but sometimes, when they were tired and hurried, or when they had long, serious conversations after the girls had gone to bed, she wondered and worried, because she knew children whose parents had stopped loving one another. Now she knew everything was all right.

Suddenly Ramona felt so happy that a book report did not seem so difficult after all—if she could think of a way to make it interesting.

The book, *The Left-Behind Cat*, which Mrs. Whaley had sent home for Ramona to read for her report, was divided into chapters but used babyish words. The story was about a cat that was left behind when a family moved away and about its adventures with a dog, another cat, and some children before it finally found a home with a nice old couple who gave it a saucer of cream and named it Lefty because its left paw was white and because it had been left behind. Medium-boring, thought Ramona, good enough to pass the time on the bus, but not good enough to read during Sustained Silent Reading. Besides, cream cost too much to give to a cat. The most the old people would give a cat was half-and-half, she thought. Ramona required accuracy from books as well as from people.

"Daddy, how do you sell something?" Ramona interrupted her father, who was studying, even though she knew she should not. However, her need for an answer was urgent.

Mr. Quimby did not look up from his book. "You ought to know. You see enough commercials on television."

Ramona considered his answer. She had always looked upon commercials as entertainment, but now she thought about some of her favorites—the cats that danced back and forth, the dog that pushed away brand-X dog food with his paw, the man who ate a pizza, got indigestion, and groaned that he couldn't believe he ate the *whole* thing, the six horses that pulled the Wells Fargo bank's stagecoach across deserts and over mountains.

"Do you mean I should do a book report like a T.V. commercial?" Ramona asked.

"Why not?" Mr. Quimby answered in an absentminded way.

"I don't want my teacher to say I'm a nuisance," said Ramona, needing assurance from a grown-up.

This time Mr. Quimby lifted his eyes from his book. "Look," he said, "she told you to pretend you're selling the book, so sell it. What better way than a T.V. commercial? You aren't being a nuisance if you do what your teacher asks." He looked at Ramona a moment and said, "Why do you worry she'd think you're a nuisance?"

Ramona stared at the carpet, wiggled her toes inside her shoes, and finally said, "I squeaked my shoes the first day of school."

"That's not being much of a nuisance," said Mr. Quimby.

"And when I got egg in my hair, Mrs. Whaley said I was a nuisance," confessed Ramona, "and then I threw up in school."

"But you didn't do those things on purpose," her father pointed out. "Now run along. I have studying to do."

Ramona thought this answer over and decided that since her parents agreed, they must be right. Well, Mrs. Whaley could just go jump in a lake, even though her teacher had written, without wasting words, that she missed her.

Ramona was going to give her book report any way she wanted. So there, Mrs. Whaley.

Ramona went to her room and looked at her table, which the family called "Ramona's studio," because it was a clutter of crayons, different kinds of paper, Scotch tape, bits of yarn, and odds and ends that Ramona used for amusing herself. Then Ramona thought a moment, and suddenly, filled with inspiration, she went to work. She knew exactly what she wanted to do and set about doing it. She worked with paper, crayons, Scotch tape, and rubber bands. She worked so hard and with such pleasure that her cheeks grew pink. Nothing in the whole world felt as good as being able to make something from a sudden idea.

Finally, with a big sigh of relief, Ramona leaned back in her chair to admire her work: three cat masks with holes for eyes and mouths, masks that could be worn by hooking rubber

bands over ears. But Ramona did not stop there. With pencil and paper, she began to write out what she would say. She was so full of ideas that she printed rather than waste time in cursive writing. Next she phoned Sara and Janet, keeping her voice low and trying not to giggle so she wouldn't disturb her father any more than necessary, and explained her plan to them. Both her friends giggled and agreed to take part in the book report. Ramona spent the rest of the evening memorizing what she was going to say.

The next morning on the bus and at school, no one even mentioned Ramona's throwing up. She had braced herself for some remark from Yard Ape, but all he said was, "Hi, Superfoot." When school started, Ramona slipped cat masks to Susan and Janet, handed her written excuse for her absence to Mrs. Whaley, and waited, fanning away escaped fruit flies, for book reports to begin.

After arithmetic, Mrs. Whaley called on several people to come to the front of the room to pretend they were selling books to the class. Most of the reports began, "This is a book about . . ." and many, as Beezus had predicted, ended with ". . . if you want to find out what happens next, read the book."

Then Mrs. Whaley said, "We have time for one more report before lunch. Who wants to be next?"

Ramona waved her hand, and Mrs. Whaley nodded.

Ramona beckoned to Sara and Janet, who giggled in an embarrassed way but joined Ramona, standing behind her and off to one side. All three girls slipped on their cat masks and giggled again. Ramona took a deep breath as Sara and Janet began to chant, "*Meow*, meow, meow, meow. *Meow*, meow, meow, meow," and danced back and forth like the cats they had seen in the cat-food commercial on television.

"*Left-Behind Cat* gives kids something to smile about," said Ramona in a loud clear voice, while her chorus meowed softly behind her. She wasn't sure that what she said was exactly true, but neither were the commercials that showed cats eating dry cat food without making any noise. "Kids who have tried *Left-Behind Cat* are all smiles, smiles, smiles. *Left-Behind*

155

Cat is the book kids ask for by name. Kids can read it every day and thrive on it. The happiest kids read *Left-Behind Cat*. *Left-Behind Cat* contains cats, dogs, people—" Here Ramona caught sight of Yard Ape leaning back in his seat, grinning in the way that always flustered her. She could not help interrupting herself with a giggle, and after suppressing it she tried not to look at Yard Ape and to take up where she had left off. ". . . cats, dogs, people—" The giggle came back, and Ramona was lost. She could not remember what came next. ". . . cats, dogs, people," she repeated, trying to start and failing.

Mrs. Whaley and the class waited. Yard Ape grinned. Ramona's loyal chorus meowed and danced. This performance could not go on all morning. Ramona had to say something, anything to end the waiting, the meowing, her book report. She tried desperately to recall a cat-food commercial, any cat-food commercial, and could

not. All she could remember was the man on television who ate the pizza, and so she blurted out the only sentence she could think of, "I can't believe I read the *whole* thing!"

Mrs. Whaley's laugh rang out above the laughter of the class. Ramona felt her face turn red behind her mask, and her ears, visible to the class, turned red as well.

"Thank you, Ramona," said Mrs. Whaley. "That was most entertaining. Class, you are excused for lunch."

Ramona felt brave behind her cat mask. "Mrs. Whaley," she said, as the class pushed back chairs and gathered up lunch boxes, "that wasn't the way my report was supposed to end."

"Did you like the book?" asked Mrs. Whaley.

"Not really," confessed Ramona.

"Then I think it was a good way to end your report," said the teacher. "Asking the class to sell books they really don't like isn't fair, now that I stop to think about it. I was only trying to make book reports a little livelier."

Encouraged by this confession and still safe behind her mask, Ramona had the boldness to speak up. "Mrs. Whaley," she said with her heart pounding, "you told Mrs. Larson that I'm a nuisance, and I don't think I am."

Mrs. Whaley looked astonished. "When did I say that?"

"The day I got egg in my hair," said Ramona. "You called me a show-off and said I was a nuisance."

Mrs. Whaley frowned, thinking. "Why, Ramona, I can recall saying something about my little show-off, but I meant it affectionately, and I'm sure I never called you a nuisance."

"Yes, you did," insisted Ramona. "You said I was a show-off, and then you said, 'What a nuisance.'" Ramona could never forget those exact words.

Mrs. Whaley, who had looked worried, smiled in relief. "Oh, Ramona, you misunderstood," she said. "I meant that trying to wash egg out of your hair was a nuisance for Mrs. Larson. I didn't mean that you personally were a nuisance."

Ramona felt a little better, enough to come out from under her mask to say, "I wasn't showing off. I was just trying to crack an egg on my head like everyone else."

Mrs. Whaley's smile was mischievous. "Tell me, Ramona," she said, "don't you ever try to show off?"

Ramona was embarrassed. "Well . . . maybe . . . sometimes, a little," she admitted. Then she added positively, "But I wasn't showing off that day. How could I be showing off when I was doing what everyone else was doing?"

"You've convinced me," said Mrs. Whaley

with a big smile. "Now run along and eat your lunch."

Ramona snatched up her lunch box and went jumping down the stairs to the cafeteria. She laughed to herself because she knew exactly what all the boys and girls from her class would say when they finished their lunches. She knew because she planned to say it herself. "I can't believe I ate the *whole* thing!"

Rainy Sunday

Rainy Sunday afternoons in November were always dismal, but Ramona felt this Sunday was the most dismal of all. She pressed her nose against the living-room window, watching the ceaseless rain pelting down as bare black branches clawed at the electric wires in front of the house. Even lunch, leftovers Mrs. Quimby had wanted to clear out of the refrigerator, had been dreary, with her parents, who seemed tired or discouraged or both, having little to say and Beezus mysteriously moody. Ramona longed for sunshine, sidewalks dry enough for roller-skating, a smiling, happy family.

"Ramona, you haven't cleaned up your room this weekend," said Mrs. Quimby, who was sitting on the couch, sorting through a stack of bills. "And don't press your nose against the window. It leaves a smudge."

Ramona felt as if everything she did was wrong. The whole family seemed cross today, even Picky-picky who meowed at the front door. With a sigh, Mrs. Quimby got up to let him out. Beezus, carrying a towel and shampoo, stalked through the living room into the kitchen, where she began to wash her hair at the sink. Mr. Quimby, studying at the dining-room table as usual, made his pencil scratch angrily across a pad of paper. The television set sat blank and mute, and in the fireplace a log sullenly refused to burn.

Mrs. Quimby sat down and then got up again as Picky-picky, indignant at the wet world outdoors, yowled to come in. "Ramona, clean up your room," she ordered, as she let the cat and a gust of cold air into the house.

"Beezus hasn't cleaned up her room." Ramona could not resist pointing this omission out to her mother.

"I'm not talking about Beezus," said Mrs. Quimby. "I'm talking about you."

Still Ramona did not move from the window. Cleaning up her room seemed such a boring thing to do, no fun at all on a rainy afternoon. She thought vaguely of all the exciting things she would like to do—learn to twirl a lariat, play a musical saw, flip around and over bars in a gymnastic competition while crowds cheered.

"Ramona, *clean up your room!*" Mrs. Quimby raised her voice.

"Well, you don't have to yell at me." Ramona's feelings were hurt by the tone of her mother's voice. The log in the fireplace settled, sending a puff of smoke into the living room.

"Then do it," snapped Mrs. Quimby. "Your room is a disaster area."

Mr. Quimby threw down his pencil. "Young lady, you do what your mother says, and you do it now. She shouldn't have to tell you three times."

"Well, all right, but you don't have to be so cross," said Ramona. To herself she thought, Nag, nag, nag.

Sulkily Ramona took her hurt feelings off to her room, where she pulled a week's collection of dirty socks from under her bed. On her way

to the bathroom hamper, she looked down the
hall and saw her sister standing in the living
room, rubbing her hair with a towel.

"Mother, I think you're mean," said Beezus
from under the towel.

Ramona stopped to listen.

"I don't care how mean you think I am," answered Mrs. Quimby. "You are not going to go,
and that is that."

"But all the other girls are going," protested
Beezus.

"I don't care if they are," said Mrs. Quimby. "You are not."

Ramona heard the sound of a pencil being slammed on the table and her father saying, "Your mother is right. Now would you kindly give me a little peace and quiet so I can get on with my work."

Beezus flounced past Ramona into her room and slammed the door. Sobs were heard, loud, angry sobs.

Where can't she go? Ramona wondered, as she dumped her socks into the hamper. Then, because she had been so good about picking up her room, Ramona returned to the living room, where Picky-picky, as cross and bored as the rest of the family, was once again meowing at the front door. "Where can't Beezus go?" she asked.

Mrs. Quimby opened the front door, and when Picky-picky hesitated, vexed by the cold wind that swept into the room, assisted him out with her toe. "She can't sleep over at Mary Jane's house with a bunch of girls from her class."

A year ago Ramona would have agreed with her mother so that her mother would love her more than Beezus, but this year she knew that she too might want to spend the night at someone's house someday. "Why can't Beezus sleep at Mary Jane's?" she asked.

"Because she comes home exhausted and grouchy." Mrs. Quimby stood by the door, waiting. Picky-picky's yowl was twisted by the wind, and when she opened the door, another cold gust swept through the house.

"With the price of fuel oil being what it is, we can't afford to let the cat out," remarked Mr. Quimby.

"Would you like to take the responsibility if I don't let him out?" asked Mrs. Quimby, before she continued with her answer to Ramona. "There are four people in the family, and she has no right to make the whole day disagreeable for the rest of us because she has been up half the night giggling with a bunch of silly girls. Besides, a growing girl needs her rest."

Ramona silently agreed with her mother about Beezus's coming home cross after such a party. At the same time, she wanted to make things easier for herself when she was in junior high school. "Maybe this time they would go to sleep earlier," she suggested.

"Fat chance," said Mrs. Quimby, who rarely spoke so rudely. "And furthermore, Ramona, Mrs. Kemp did not come right out and say so, but she did drop a hint that you are not playing as nicely with Willa Jean as you might."

Ramona heaved a sigh that seemed to come from the soles of her feet. In the bedroom, Beezus, who had run out of real sobs, was working hard to force out fake sobs to show her parents how mean they were to her.

169

Mrs. Quimby ignored the sighs and the sobs and continued. "Ramona, you know that getting along at the Kemps' is your job in this family. I've told you that before."

How could Ramona explain to her mother that Willa Jean had finally caught on that Sustained Silent Reading was just plain reading a book? For a while, Willa Jean wanted Ramona to read aloud a few boring books the Kemps owned, the sort of books people who did not know anything about children so often gave them. Willa Jean listened to them several times, grew bored, and now insisted on playing beauty shop. Ramona did not want her fingernails painted by Willa Jean and knew she would be blamed if Willa Jean spilled nail polish. Instead of Mrs. Kemp's taking care of Ramona, Ramona was taking care of Willa Jean.

Ramona looked at the carpet, sighed again, and said, "I try." She felt sorry for herself, misunderstood and unappreciated. Nobody in the whole world understood how hard it was to go to the Kemps' house after school when she did not have a bicycle.

Mrs. Quimby relented. "I know it isn't easy," she said with a half smile, "but don't give up." She gathered up the bills and checkbook and went into the kitchen, where she began to write checks at the kitchen table.

Ramona wandered into the dining room to seek comfort from her father. She laid her cheek against the sleeve of his plaid shirt and asked, "Daddy, what are you studying?"

Once again Mr. Quimby threw down his pencil. "I am studying the cognitive processes of children," he answered.

Ramona raised her head to look at him. "What does that mean?" she asked.

"How kids think," her father told her.

Ramona did not like the sound of this subject

171

at all. "Why are you studying *that*?" she demanded. Some things should be private, and how children thought was one of them. She did not like the idea of grown-ups snooping around in thick books trying to find out.

"That is exactly what I have been asking myself." Mr. Quimby was serious. "Why am I studying this stuff when we have bills to pay?"

"Well, I don't think you should," said Ramona. "It's none of your business how kids think." Then she quickly added, because she did not want her father to drop out of school and be a checker again, "There are lots of other things you could study. Things like fruit flies."

Mr. Quimby smiled at Ramona and rumpled her hair. "I doubt if anyone could figure out how you think," he said, which made Ramona feel better, as if her secret thoughts were still safe.

Mr. Quimby sat gnawing his pencil and staring out the window at the rain. Beezus, who had

run out of fake sobs, emerged from her room, red-eyed and damp-haired, to stalk about the house not speaking to anyone.

Ramona flopped down on the couch. She hated rainy Sundays, especially this one, and longed for Monday when she could escape to school. The Quimbys' house seemed to have grown smaller during the day until it was no longer big enough to hold her family and all its problems. She tried not to think of the half-overheard conversations of her parents after the

girls had gone to bed, grown-up talk that Ramona understood just enough to know her parents were concerned about their future.

Ramona had deep, secret worries of her own.
She worried that her father might accidentally
be locked in the frozen-food warehouse, where
it was so cold it sometimes snowed indoors.
What if he was filling a big order, and the men
who were lucky enough to get small orders to
fill left work ahead of him and forgot and locked
the warehouse, and he couldn't get out and froze
to death? Of course that wouldn't happen. "But
it might," insisted a tiny voice in the back of her
mind. Don't be silly, she told the little voice.
"Yes, but—" began the little voice. And despite
the worry that would not go away Ramona
wanted her father to go on working so he could
stay in school and someday get a job he liked.

While Ramona worried, the house was silent
except for the sound of rain and the scratch of

her father's pencil. The smoking log settled in the fireplace, sending up a few feeble sparks. The day grew darker, Ramona was beginning to feel hungry, but there was no comfortable bustle of cooking in the kitchen.

Suddenly Mr. Quimby slammed shut his book and threw down his pencil so hard it bounced onto the floor. Ramona sat up. Now what was wrong?

"Come on, everybody," said her father. "Get cleaned up. Let's stop this grumping around. We are going out for dinner, and we are going to smile and be pleasant if it kills us. That's an order!"

The girls stared at their father and then at one another. What was going on? They had not gone out to dinner for months, so how could they afford to go now?

"To the Whopperburger?" asked Ramona.

"Sure," said Mr. Quimby, who appeared cheerful for the first time that day. "Why not? The sky's the limit."

Mrs. Quimby came into the living room with a handful of stamped envelopes. "But Bob—" she began.

"Now don't worry," her husband said. "We'll manage. During Thanksgiving I'll be putting in more hours in the warehouse and getting more overtime. There's no reason why we can't have a treat once in a while. And the Whopperburger isn't exactly your four-star gourmet restaurant."

Ramona was afraid her mother might give a lecture on the evils of junk food, but she did not. Gloom and anger were forgotten. Clothes were changed, hair combed, Picky-picky was shut in the basement, and the family was on its way in the old car with the new transmission that never balked at backing down the driveway. Off the Quimbys sped to the nearest Whopperburger, where they discovered other families must have wanted to get out of the house on a rainy day, for the restaurant was crowded, and they had to wait for a table.

There were enough chairs for the grown-ups and Beezus, but Ramona, who had the youngest legs, had to stand up. She amused herself by punching the buttons on the cigarette machine in time to the Muzak, which was playing "Tie a Yellow Ribbon 'Round the Old Oak Tree." She even danced a little to the music, and, when the tune came to an end, she turned around and found herself face to face with an old man with neatly trimmed gray hair and a moustache that turned up at the ends. He was dressed as if everything he wore—a flowered shirt, striped tie, tweed coat and plaid slacks—had come from different stores or from a rummage sale, except that the crease in his trousers was sharp and his shoes were shined.

The old man, whose back was very straight,

saluted Ramona as if she were a soldier and said, "Well, young lady, have you been good to your mother?"

Ramona was stunned. She felt her face turn red to the tips of her ears. She did not know how to answer such a question. Had she been good to her mother? Well . . . not always, but why was this stranger asking? It was none of his business. He had no right to ask such a question.

Ramona looked to her parents for help and discovered they were waiting with amusement for her answer. So were the rest of the people who were waiting for tables. Ramona scowled at the man. She did not have to answer him if she did not want to.

The hostess saved Ramona by calling out, "Quimby, party of four," and leading the family to a plastic-upholstered booth.

"Why didn't you answer the man?" Beezus was as amused as everyone else.

"I'm not supposed to talk to strangers," was Ramona's dignified answer.

"But Mother and Daddy are with us," Beezus pointed out, rather meanly, Ramona thought.

"Remember," said Mr. Quimby, as he opened his menu, "we are all going to smile and enjoy ourselves if it kills us."

As Ramona picked up her menu, she was still seething inside. Maybe she hadn't always been good to her mother, but that man had no right to pry. When she discovered he was seated in a single booth across the aisle, she gave him an indignant look, which he answered with a merry wink. So he had been teasing. Well, Ramona didn't like it.

When Ramona opened her menu, she made an exciting discovery. She no longer had to depend on colored pictures of hamburgers, French fries, chili, and steak to help her make up her mind. She could now read what was offered. She stud-

ied carefully, and when she came to the bottom
of the menu, she read the dreaded words,
"Child's Plate for Children Under Twelve." Then
came the list of choices: fish sticks, chicken
drumsticks, hot dogs. None of them, to Ramona,
food for a treat. They were food for a school
cafeteria.

"Daddy," Ramona whispered, "do I have to
have a child's plate?"

"Not if you don't want to." Her father's smile
was understanding. Ramona ordered the small-
est adult item on the menu.

Whopperburger was noted for fast service,
and in a few minutes the waitress set down the
Quimbys' dinners: a hamburger and French
fries for Ramona, a cheeseburger and French
fries for Beezus and her mother, and hamburgers
with chili for her father.

Ramona bit into her hamburger. Bliss. Warm,
soft, juicy, tart with relish. Juice dribbled down

her chin. She noticed her mother start to say something and change her mind. Ramona caught the dribble with her paper napkin before it reached her collar. The French fries—crisp on the outside, mealy on the inside—tasted better than anything Ramona had ever eaten.

The family ate in companionable silence for a few moments until the edge was taken off their hunger. "A little change once in a while does make a difference," said Mrs. Quimby. "It does us all good."

"Especially after the way—" Ramona stopped herself from finishing with, "—after the way Beezus acted this afternoon." Instead she sat up straight and smiled.

"Well, I wasn't the only one who—" Beezus also stopped in midsentence and smiled. The parents looked stern, but they managed to smile. Suddenly everyone relaxed and laughed.

The old man, Ramona noticed, was eating a

steak. She wished her father could afford a steak.

As much as she enjoyed her hamburger, Ramona was unable to finish. It was too much. She was happy when her mother did not say, "Someone's eyes are bigger than her stomach." Her father, without commenting on the unfinished hamburger, included her in the orders of apple pie with hot cinnamon sauce and ice cream.

Ramona ate what she could, and after watching the ice cream melt into the cinnamon sauce, she glanced over at the old man, who was having a serious discussion with the waitress. She seemed surprised and upset about something. The Muzak, conversation of other customers, and rattle of dishes made eavesdropping impossible. The waitress left. Ramona saw her speak to the manager, who listened and then nodded. For a moment Ramona thought the man might not have enough money to pay for the steak he

183

had eaten. Apparently he did, however, for after
listening to what the waitress had to say, he left
a tip under the edge of his plate and picked up
his check. To Ramona's embarrassment, he
stood up, winked, and saluted her again. Then
he left. Ramona did not know what to make of
him.

She turned back to her family, whose smiles

were now genuine rather than determined. The sight of them gave her courage to ask the question that had been nibbling at the back of her mind, "Daddy, you aren't going to be a college dropout, are you?"

Mr. Quimby finished a mouthful of pie before he answered, "Nope."

Ramona wanted to make sure. "And you won't ever be a checker and come home cross again?"

"Well," said her father, "I can't promise I won't come home cross, but if I do, it won't be from standing at the cash register trying to remember forty-two price changes in the produce section while a long line of customers, all in a hurry, wait to pay for their groceries."

Ramona was reassured.

When the waitress descended on the Quimbys to offer the grown-ups a second cup of coffee, Mr. Quimby said, "Check, please."

The waitress looked embarrassed. "Well . . .

a . . ." She hesitated. "This has never happened before, but your meals have already been paid for."

The Quimbys looked at her in astonishment. "But who paid for them?" demanded Mr. Quimby.

"A lonely gentleman who left a little while ago," answered the waitress.

"He must have been the man who sat across the aisle," said Mrs. Quimby. "But why would he pay for our dinners? We never saw him before in our lives."

The waitress smiled. "Because he said you are such a nice family, and because he misses his children and grandchildren." She dashed off with her pot of coffee, leaving the Quimbys in surprised, even shocked, silence. A nice family? After the way they had behaved on a rainy Sunday.

"A mysterious stranger just like in a book," said Beezus. "I never thought I'd meet one."

"Poor lonely man," said Mrs. Quimby at last, as Mr. Quimby shoved a tip under his saucer. Still stunned into silence, the family struggled into their wraps and splashed across the parking lot to their car, which started promptly and backed obediently out of its parking space. As the windshield wipers began their rhythmic exercise, the family rode in silence, each thinking of the events of the day.

"You know," said Mrs. Quimby thoughtfully, as the car left the parking lot and headed down the street, "I think he was right. We are a nice family."

"Not all the time," said Ramona, as usual demanding accuracy.

"Nobody is nice all the time," answered her father. "Or if they are, they are boring."

187

"Not even your parents are nice all the time," added Mrs. Quimby.

Ramona secretly agreed, but she had not expected her parents to admit it. Deep down inside, she felt she herself was nice all the time, but sometimes on the outside her niceness sort of—well, curdled. Then people did not understand how nice she really was. Maybe other people curdled too.

"We have our ups and downs," said Mrs. Quimby, "but we manage to get along, and we stick together."

"We are nicer than some families I know," said Beezus. "Some families don't even eat dinner together." After a moment she made a confession. "I don't really like sleeping on someone's floor in a sleeping bag."

"I didn't think you did." Mrs. Quimby reached back and patted Beezus on the knee. "That's

one reason I said you couldn't go. You didn't
want to go, but didn't want to admit it."

Ramona snuggled inside her car coat, feeling
cozy enclosed in the car with the heater breath-
ing warm air on her nice family. She was a member of a nice sticking-together family, and she
was old enough to be depended upon, so she
could ignore—or at least try to ignore—a lot of

things. Willa Jean—she would try reading her Sustained Silent Reading books aloud because Willa Jean was old enough to understand most of them. That should work for a little while. Mrs. Whaley—some things were nice about her and some were not. Ramona could get along.

"That man paying for our dinner was sort of like a happy ending," remarked Beezus, as the family, snug in their car, drove through the rain and the dark toward Klickitat Street.

"A happy ending for today," corrected Ramona. Tomorrow they would begin all over again.

ABOUT THE AUTHOR

Beverly Cleary was born in a small town in Oregon, where she lived until she reached school age. At that time her family moved to Portland, where she went to grammar and high school. After graduating from the University of California at Berkeley, she entered the School of Librarianship at the University of Washington in Seattle, specializing in library work with children. In 1939 she became Children's Librarian in Yakima, Washington.

In 1940 she married Clarence T. Cleary, and they moved to Oakland, California. During World War II Mrs. Cleary was Post Librarian at the Oakland Army Hospital. The Clearys now live in Carmel. They are the parents of twins, a boy and girl.

copy #7

JUV
FIC
CLE   Cleary, Beverly

         Ramona Quimby,
         age 8

DATE DUE

JUN. 20 1992	JY 24 '99	
JUL. 6 1992	JUL 03 2003	
SEP. 24 1992	NOV 08 2004	
JUL. 21 1994	AP 05 '06	
	SE 18 '08	
OCT. 1 5 1994		
OCT. 19 1995	JY 13 '09	
FE 13 '97	FE 2 7 '10	
JY 15 '97	OC 2 3 '10	
FE 24 '99		